# I'VE BEEN WAITING

# Other Titles by Jack Lawrence

~

Blood Thorn
Bed of Thorns

# I'VE BEEN WAITING

# Jack Lawrence

# I'VE BEEN WAITING

# Jack Lawrence

# Prologue

*The stab wound in her shoulder seemed to bleed more. The burning within her flesh intensified with the rage of an uncontrollable flame, spreading through her upper body with reckless abandon. As her heart hammered more, her lungs fought for air. Between the sprinting, the stab wound, and the terror, she couldn't catch her breath.*

*Darkness had set upon the forest over thirty minutes before he stabbed her. She never saw it coming. Why would she? She trusted him completely. He was one of the few people she could confide her darkest truths to. What was even more agonizing had been the absence of any warnings. He leaned in to kiss her. As she closed her eyes, preparing for her first kiss—thoughts of romance along with the anticipation for the big moment racing through her mind—she instead felt the crippling pain of the steel entering her shoulder. She saw his eyes then.*

*Empty.*
*Cold.*
*Hungry.*

*She kicked him in the groin, then ran after he forced the blade from her shoulder to strike again. Her father had always told her,* "If a man grabs you, go for the balls. When you feel you are in danger, it will stop the threat just about every time. When your life is in danger, you only get one chance." *Oh, God, her father! What would happen to him if she did not come home? How would he make it through if her lifeless body were to be found in the woods?*

*She sought asylum behind a large fallen tree where she crawled under overgrowth that spread across the log and onto other trees. It created a camouflaged blind in which she could see in the direction she had come. A sizable boulder shielded her from the rear, in case he had circled trying to cut her off. She held her breath for a moment, which hurt less than trying to breathe.*

*Her mind returned to her father. She was all he had left. Ever since her mother had overdosed the year before. In six months, she would start college—he was so proud of her for that. She selected one less than two hours from home so she could stay with him. So, he wouldn't lose her, too. If she were honest, she knew, so she couldn't lose him. She wished he were there with her to make this all stop. He had always been her shield.*

*She heard his voice again.* You are the bravest woman I know, honey. Anyone who messes with you has no idea what kind of hurt they're signing up for.

*He was right. She felt around in the dirt with her left arm, moving slowly so she would not make too much noise. Even with the full moon, her hiding spot rested in darkness from the overgrown foliage. She grabbed a handful of dirt and began massaging it over her face and her black hair. Once she felt her face was covered adequately, she felt around for a weapon, her eyes still glued to the direction she had come from. She could hear him running through the woods. He was getting closer.*

*All she found was a rock the size of her fist. She decided it would have to do. She took a deep breath forcing herself to bite her lip at the sudden shot of pain that nearly knocked her out of consciousness. Her head began to throb with the intensity of a kick drum. Her eyes suddenly felt heavier. Then, she saw him emerge from the trees.*

*He had come to a stop twenty yards from her concealed position and surveyed the surroundings. An eerie stillness had settled over the woods, as if the nocturnal creatures could sense the presence of malevolence and had retreated to their own shelters. Even the leaves seemed to pause their rustling. She had glimpsed his eyes, once filled with tenderness and radiance, now laser-focused with something malignant.*

*"Come out to play! Since you are my first, I will do you a favor; I'll make the game quick."*

*Her eyes were awake now. The throbbing heat in her arm subsided. Her heart rate picked up which worried her. The faster her heart beat, the faster she would bleed out. It hurt too much to take deep breaths, even if she could, she knew it would not help her there.*

*Her father's voice came for a third—and final—time.* Do you know why we chose your name? Because it has several beautiful meanings. Immortal, promised by God, and strength. I swear nothing could describe you better.

*He moved to his right, just out of her view from her hiding spot. She considered lifting her head for just a moment to see if she could spot where he had gone. She quickly decided against it. He would certainly find her then.*

*A deeper—more complete—silence draped itself over the forest. It became more suffocating with each passing moment. She could not hear him walking or breathing. She did not know if it meant he had left or if he had simply stopped moving.*

*Then the roof of her hideaway collapsed under a great weight as something heavy landed on her. Something breathing. Something pressed cold metal violently to the back of her neck. Then she recognized it was* him, *he had found her. He was going to end her life..*

# 1

Amari Richards awoke abruptly, her body drenched in a frigid sweat. It was clear the sweat came from the nightmare rather than the heat of the summer night. Her hand clenched at her right shoulder as the pain radiated outward, a pain she thought would never return. Then again, she thought the nightmares had ended long ago, as well.

She rolled free from the tangled sheets and then hurried to the bathroom. Her stomach churned with flashes from the nightmare replaying in her mind, gradually fading away—though never vanishing fully. His once deep-set blue eyes turned soulless that night in the woods. His short brown hair nearly vanished against the dark backdrop of the woods. His athletic body, effortlessly moved through the darkness of the forest. His heart-melting smile turned malevolent when he drew the knife… The memory was permanent.

Amari splashed cold water over her face, washing away the remnants of sleep and dread from her face. The shock of the cold jolted her into alertness. By the time she reached for the towel, what little memory of the nightmare she'd had dissipated. Still, she could visualize the event as clearly now as when she lived through it.

She could see her father's face when he first stepped into her room at the hospital. There'd been a week-long search for Samael Skinner's body after she had bashed the rock into his temple, though they never found him. The dogs had tracked Samael's blood toward Sugar Creek, but after two weeks of torrential rains, the ravenous river swallowed up much that crossed its path. The police believed Samael had also been consumed by it, especially given his head injury, which would have likely left him uneasy on his feet and disoriented. However, some fluttering discontent told her they were wrong. The thought had not bothered her for a long time. Not until now.

The surgery, followed by months of recuperation and the demanding physical therapy for her shoulder's healing, were experiences she'd never forget. Nor would she forget the nights she woke up screaming, with her father, James Richardson, by her side, a shotgun in hand, ensuring she could sleep through the night. His wavy brown hair fell over his ears like frayed wires. His squared jaw clenched so tightly that the muscles beneath his skin would twitch frantically. His deep brown eyes carried a mixture of hopelessness and yearning. His powerful farmer's body had weathered more after her assault than it ever did tending to the fields. About a week after her return, he'd experienced a burst of optimism that gradually pulled her out of the dark pit where she found herself.

Perhaps it was what drove her so hard. In her work, she hardly found any time for her mind to wander to the old haunting thoughts of that night of reckoning near her family home in New Hope, Indiana. Now here she was, preparing to go back home for the first time since she had left to attend IU. Her father even relocated to a small town just north of Bloomington. An attempt to escape his own ghosts just as much she had. He had kept their old cabin in hopes of one day returning as a family, though now, that dream, like many, had been shattered.

Amari had decided to take her first vacation in nearly three years so she could go back to New Hope to help her father prepare the house for sale. Time to do something different, perhaps something less stressful. Mostly, she knew to spend time with her father. She finally scheduled the trip three months ago. A week later, her father died at the cabin. Massive heart attack. He had been buried next to her mother. Now she would be making the trip unaccompanied. The thought plagued her with guilt. She missed the burial because she couldn't bring herself to go back home then. Now, she would, except she would be doing it alone.

After graduating from IU with a degree in criminal justice, Amari immediately joined the Indianapolis Metropolitan Police Department. She knew she could be a voice for victims; the nightmares she ran from drowned in her work which was what she came to love about her twelve-hour shifts. Within two years, she took the detective exam and was promoted to detective for the Violent Crime Unit—the youngest female to do so at only twenty-five years old. Four years later, at the age of twenty-nine, she decided she could do more. She loved the job as well as the officers she served with, yet there was an emptiness she never could put a finger on. Then, when her former partner Laramy Hathaway offered her a full partnership in his business—Blackout Security and Investigative Services—she could not resist.

For the past five years, she'd been heading the investigative unit of the business. Luckily, business was good. The olive-skinned girl from the small town no one ever escaped was now making six figures providing security and private investigator services to politicians, athletes, and lawyers looking for extra dirt to reinforce the foundations of their cases. She had a lot to be proud of. Her father reminded her every time they had spoken, one of the many things she missed about talking to him. Still, he had always wished to see her more over the years. He had wished she would have visited more. She worked *too* hard.

He had been right. As she stared at a reflection she scarcely recognized, she could only count ten—maybe twelve—times she had seen her father over the past six years. Now, he was gone. Her first vacation in years, the opportunity to atone for her absence, he would not be there. Amari would be preparing the house for sale on her own. She considered canceling, but Laramy wouldn't have it. He even threatened to change the locks to the building and lock her out of the system.

"I'll have security throw you out. I will toss your ass out myself if I have to. You deserve a break, Mari. Even if you don't go there, you need to go somewhere. Relax, unwind, do something stupid!"

She laughed at the thought. She would drive a little more than ninety minutes west, then spend the next week and a half in the house where her nightmares began. Where her life was nearly stolen from her. Where secrets had been buried alongside her father, a few hundred feet from the empty grave of Samael Skinner—which had been marked with minimal fanfare—in New Hope Cemetery. She only hoped she could get in and out a little more relaxed and without any of the ghosts of her past clawing their way out.

# 2

Amari spent an hour packing the last of her toiletries along with extra clothes, lugging them down the stairs of her condo before then heaving them into her trunk. Even though she had only planned to stay a week, she packed for two. One lesson she had learned repeatedly throughout her life was to always be prepared. As her dad always said, "Two is one, one is none."

After she double checked she had put her luggage in the trunk, she had checked to ensure each window to the house was latched, each electronic device was unplugged, and that the food dispenser for her cat, Glover—a name earned by the two jet black front paws which contrasted against his glowing white fur—was full to the brim, she sat on the couch to delay her departure a little longer. Despite knowing her neighbor Janet would be checking on the cat every other day. Amari didn't know the woman well, but she always brought Glover a new toy or cat nip-filled ball. Amari felt comfortable letting the woman check in on the cat, especially since her home had nothing worth stealing.

She removed her phone from her front pocket so she could call Laramy. It rang only once before the scratchy voice answered. In her mind, she could see his large left hand with only half his thumb ruffling through his graying beard. He would have been removing his glasses before rubbing his blue eyes violently with the same callused hand as if threatening the fatigue away.

"Weren't you supposed to be on the road fifteen minutes ago?"

Amari sighed, fully expecting the question. "I was. I am stalling."

"You can't come back to work for two weeks. You are on vacation." She could hear him biting back a smile. "So, you really have no choice. Might as well just go."

"I know," she told him. "I'm just… It's been a long time since I've been back home."

Laramy lowered his voice, the teasing tone giving way to a tone much more supportive. "I can always sneak away for a day or two. Just until you feel comfortable. Just say the word, partner. You know I'm there."

Amari smiled as she felt herself warm. Laramy had become like an unofficial uncle to her. On her second day, she and Laramy had been assigned partners at IMPD. Once, he shoved her to the ground when a suspect fired two shots at them. Now, he was still wanting to protect her from the monsters residing in her head. He was there the same way her father always had been. Even though she could defend herself, it felt nice knowing someone still had her back.

"I appreciate you, Laramy. You know as well as I do that this is something I have to do myself."

"Then get your skinny ass in the car so you can get moving."

Amari laughed and felt her tension subside. "Thanks, Laramy. I'll give you a call when I get into town."

She hung up then slowly made her way through the house one last time. If she didn't know it was her house, she could have sworn it had been abandoned. The house looked lonely, she thought, looking at it for the final time. No character, nothing that said it belonged to her. Of course, she wasn't home often. And she wasn't sure she herself had anything to add to the bare walls to make it a *home*.

Amari left when she had no more excuses and nothing left to check. She gave the doorknob two tugs from the outside before she allowed herself to go to her car.

The first twenty minutes of the drive felt like it passed at a snail's pace. Each mile seemed to take three times as long as it should. Between construction, traffic, and her nerves, she felt her mind begin to race. She reached for the radio dial and tapped the screen, turning it on.

Most people at the office made it a point to razz her about being one of the only people left in the world to listen to the radio. While most had downloaded music apps or audiobooks, Amari found comfort in the nostalgia of FM radio.

"Another body has been discovered," a relaxed female voice said over the airwaves in a matter-of-fact voice that said it was just business as usual. "The victim was an eighteen-year-old female whose identity has not been released. However, police say the scene matches that of six other young female victims found in various forests from Michigan down to Georgia. Police…"

Amari turned off the radio while forcing her car to the side of the interstate. Her heart had been hammering against her chest. She noticed her mouth had suddenly gone desert dry. She tried to control her breathing, but it was beginning to run away from her. She felt the world around her shrinking like a lid would be closed on top of her. Breathing became a labored event.

She made it a point to not follow the recent string of killings—which bore a frightening closeness to her experience. Seven victims. It had only been four two weeks earlier. They were moving fast, and she didn't think they would be slowing down. As far as she could tell, each victim had been seventeen or eighteen, always female with dark hair. They had also all stemmed from a single-parent home. Each one was found stabbed and then dragged near a body of water in the woods. As much as she tried to tell herself otherwise, she had known.

Instinctively she knew who the I-65 Killer was.

It was *him*.

# 3

The weight on top of her felt suffocating. It caused the pain in Amari's shoulder to explode through her chest like shrapnel. When she felt the cold steel of the knife against the back of her neck, she froze, and the sweetness of his breath caused her muscles to lock. He grabbed her hair and pulled up and left forcing her whole body to follow. Before she could move, the knife was at her throat. His eyes stared into hers. When he saw the fear in them, he smiled.

Amari felt the rough surface of the rock still clutched in her hand. She could feel his knees digging into her thighs, forcing them to remain still. His left elbow dug into her right arm, but her left was free. She swung the rock in her left hand as hard as she could. When it connected with the side of his head, a sickening crunch seemed to echo off the surrounding forest. The resonant howl was stiffened by his animalistic wail of pain.

He rolled free from her, but Amari felt stuck as she struggled to stand. She realized his hand was still tightly grasped around her wrist. Amari sat up the best she could then brought the rock down again, this time striking the top of his wrist. He let go of her allowing her to stand to run.

Something hard crashed into her right leg, causing it to tangle with her left. Amari plummeted to the ground sending the rock—her sole source of protection and refuge—flying from her grasp. She could hear it tumbling through the foliage before her. As she tried to figure out what had tripped her, she felt him on top of her again.

*"That is not how we play this game!" his words were gently slurred but clear enough.*

*He pulled her head up by the hair again, this time sliding the knife under her neck. He lowered her head slightly. Amari could sense his face behind her. She flung her head back as fast as she could, forcing a* crack *sound to ring out with another deafening scream. Amari's head buzzed as stars danced around in her eyes. A sudden flood of nausea swayed in her stomach. Then, as soon as she felt the weight of him fall from her back, she stood up.*

*Amari had no intention of trying to run again. He lay there, writhing in pain. She would end this. He would not get another chance to attack her. Bending down, she grabbed a log slightly thicker than her arm. The pain in her shoulder faded to not much more than a dull ache, her breathing was labored, but even the burning in her lungs had mostly subsided.*

*Amari heaved the log up as high above her head as she could. Then Amari brought it down with her body weight behind it. Three loud thuds resonated through the forest. On her fourth swing, the log splintered leaving nothing in her grasp. Amari forced herself to glance down at him. He was not breathing. He was not crying in pain. He was motionless. Completely still.*

*She turned with a snap of her body, forcing her legs to spin, praying whatever direction she was running in would lead her to safety. She knew the river lay hidden somewhere behind her. Except, she couldn't remember if the two of them had been on the north side—which led to the road—or the south—which would lead her deeper into the endless acres of forest.*

*After what seemed like hours of running, a shimmering hope of light from the full moon reflected from asphalt. Bursting from the tree line, Amari felt every bit of pain her adrenaline had forced down during her final stand. She collapsed onto the cool pavement and began dry heaving. Half a moment later, her nausea was interrupted by a pair of bright lights which temporarily blinded her. She tried to waive, uncertain if she was or if it was a phantom feeling, her mind and body nearly entirely disconnected. Her arm had gone numb again from the stab wound, and her heart was thunderous.*

*An engine purred to rest, followed by the slam of a metal door and the weight of heavy footsteps pounding on the concrete. She screamed when the strong hands grabbed her shoulders. Then she heard the frightened voice of a man.*

*"Jesus Christ, you're bleedin' everywhere."*

*"He stabbed... he stabbed me..."*

*"Who? Where is he?" the man's twang seemed stronger than most people she knew in town. She found it comforting. Almost reassuring.*

*Amari pointed with her left hand into the woods. The numbness paralyzed her right arm, causing her to fold onto the pavement as it crumbled beneath her. The man picked her up with one fluid motion before he carried her to the truck. He lifted her onto the bed. As her eyes gained clarity, she was able to take in her liberator's appearance. He was older than her, maybe her dad's age. Random patches of white peppered his goatee and along the front of his hairline, which had begun to backtrack from its original placement. His hair was short, although not short enough to conceal the specks of white. He wore what everyone there wore, jeans and a flannel shirt. He boasted laugh lines around his eyes like her dad. Like a man who laughed a lot. Though at that moment, his face had been ashen, devoid of the usual smile. His green eyes promised safety.*

*"Where is he?" the man asked again.*

*"I don't... I don't know. Straight back near a fallen tree."*

*The man pulled a Samsung flip phone from his pocket. "Call the police. Tell them you need help at mile marker thirteen." He then pulled a knife from his pocket, flipped it open, and handed it to her. "If he comes back, use this!"*

*She watched as the man opened the back door of his truck, where he pulled a shotgun out. He racked one shell into the chamber, giving her one final glance before heading for the tree line.*

*"No!" She cried. "Don't leave me here!"*

*"Call the police. I'll be right back."*

*When the darkness consumed him, she dialed 9-1-1. She told the operator exactly what the man had said, and then as the operator tried to keep her talking, Amari felt the world close in around her. The pain grew to unbearable levels as blackness beckoned to her. It was a strangely comforting sensation. Had this been what her mother had felt?*

*Unaware of how much time had passed by since the darkness had temporarily claimed her, she was pulled back by the wails of sirens and the man talking to her. When her eyes fluttered back to life, she found herself in a circle of paramedics attaching her to a longboard, edged by two police officers and the man who had saved her.*

*"Did you find him? Is he alive?" she asked the man.*

*"No," he told her as he turned to a nameless officer. "I didn't see anyone. I found some blood, though. I tracked it back to the river. Couldn't see much, it's flooded something nasty. Wouldn't be surprised if it swept him on off somewhere."*

*If he had not found Samael, he was not dead. If he wasn't dead, he would be back for her.*

*As the paramedics slid her into the back of an ambulance, an officer climbed in with her. "I am going to stay by your side the whole time. You're safe now, I promise."*

*Amari believed her.*

*"I just need you to tell me everything you remember. Do you know who did this?"*

*Amari nodded her head as the doors to the ambulance were closed, she watched the man follow the other officer back into the woods.*

*"Who was he? The man who found me?"*

*"John Meadowbrook."*

# 4

Amari's trance was shattered by the blaring horn of a passing car. The driver of the car—an old man who reminded her of Walter Matthau except grumpier—presented his middle finger high in her direction. She scoffed at the gesture as she checked her mirrors to confirm she had indeed pulled over to the shoulder to be out of the line of traffic.

Amari drew in a deep breath before pulling away from the shoulder of the highway before any other angry drivers decided to grace her with their rage. A half mile later, she found a rest stop to turn into. She parked her car under a large willow tree, shaded from the summer sun.

Closing her eyes, Amari ran a shaking hand over her face. The images were becoming more vivid the closer she got to home, even though she was still over half an hour away.

"Why didn't you just go to Hawaii?" she asked herself out loud. Even in her solitude, she felt ashamed by the tremble in her voice. Almost weekly, she was cold-called by supposed investors offering cash for her family's property. She could have sold it to them and let them deal with the whole process while she sipped a Mai Tai on the beach before a night of regrettable passion with a stranger she would never have to open up to. She cursed herself for not having done so.

Vulnerability was the impenetrable wall between her and any meaningful relationship. As soon as a man asked her about her childhood, where she grew up, or what drove her to become a cop, she'd shut down, constructing a new layer to the wall with a new reason he was wrong for her. Sometimes she even convinced herself of its truth.

"Stop it!" Her own voice surprised her. She looked into the rearview mirror to meet her weary gaze. "You have been shot at, fought killers and men three times your size. That shit was twenty years ago! You are not the same petrified, defenseless seventeen-year-old girl in the woods. Stop it!"

She took a deep breath, continuing the internal conversation. *You've been through it. You* have *dealt with it. You can clean out a house, dammit. Get it together.*

Amari opened the center console where her arm had been resting, freeing her Smith & Wesson M&P Shield chambered in 9mm. A sudden wash of relief cleansed her. In thirty minutes, she would be back home. Whether the ghosts of her past were still there or not, she knew she would be able to face them.

She was right—she was not the same scared girl she had been twenty years ago. She was trained and proficient in self-defense. She survived that night; now it was time to go back home. Nothing and no one could hurt her there now. Especially not now.

Amari exited her car to go into the rest area, passing the Indiana maps lining the walls before heading straight to the vending machine. She got a Coke, gulping from the can as quickly as she could. The cold liquid burned the back of her throat. Though it was not a Mai Tai, it was refreshing. Once she finished it, she went into the bathroom. Amari ran cold water over her face to shock away the trepidation.

She wasn't entirely sure if she believed her pep talk, but she could not waste any more time. In just over thirty minutes, she'd be pulling into the driveway of her childhood home. A home nestled in a town where her innocence had been stolen, along with her naive view of the world. The town where her dreams of becoming a photographer died and the life-long mission of never being a victim again, had been born. It was the place she spent her entire adult life running from. Only to be in that moment, finding herself forced to return. Forced to confront everything she had hoped to leave behind. She was on a head-on course with a runaway train. But she would face it—as she always did—and whatever came with it.

# 5

Amari continued driving down State Road 236, nearing New Hope. Her stomach knotted up again. She reached the cemetery just a few miles outside of downtown—a term used much more loosely since seeing the downtowns of major cities—where her mother and father were buried. Only a hundred yards from the marker of Samael Skinner. She pulled into the cemetery finding herself surrounded by cornfields. Even with the sun shining, unobstructed by any trees or clouds, she felt a darkness come over her.

Amari parked at the end of the main road, where it forked in two directions. From her position, she could see the grassless spot where her father's grave rested. The tombstone hadn't yet been updated with her father's inscription, which frustrated her.

She walked slowly to her parent's resting place. Her feet trudging as if the dying blades of grass were gripping her to pull her down for sustenance, clearly a drought had deprived them for far too long. For the first time since the phone call from the hospital, she knew how alone she was in the world. Her father was the only family she had left, one of the few people she could call on when the day had been particularly rough. She wished he were there now. He would have made the trip home bearable.

Safer.

At the headstone, she lowered herself to her knees, her hand on the top of the granite. She looked to the left, where her mother's name had been etched years before. "Hi, Mom."

She lowered herself completely, her hand never leaving the stone. Her father's name was etched in the stone, something he had done when ordering the marking for his wife. Her frustration reawakened at not seeing either the date of death or the Bible verse Amari had ordered when he died.

Amari put her palm on the smooth surface of the granite under her father's name.

"Hey, Dad. Looks like I finally made it back..." Guilt flooded through her again. "Sorry, I wasn't here for the funeral. It's hard coming back here. I miss you so much."

Amari shifted her body to move her knees from underneath her, her hand still on the stone. "I am thankful you left me the cabin, but I also wish you hadn't. I really don't want to be back here, especially without you. I just hope I can make it through and get the house sold soon."

She shook her head. "Sorry, I know how much you loved the house. I'm still single with no real prospects. Not that it would matter. I'm so busy with work, I don't have much time for a love life."

Amari sat silently for several minutes, listening to birds singing in the distance as if everything in the world were right, oblivious to the torment unfolding inside of her. After a long inhale, Amari leaned in to kiss the granite where her father's name had been etched. As she reached her feet, she looked to her mother's name staring back at her; *Stacy.* "Bye, Mom," she said before turning back toward her car.

This was it. No more stops. No more detours. In two miles, she would be pulling into downtown before taking the main road toward the way to the family cabin. The memories of her former life would come flooding back to her. Amari knew there was nothing she could do to stop it. She had to face it. She was home again. As much as she hated the idea of it, she had returned to the place she blamed for every bad memory, every nightmare she had ever had. The place where her mother died, where she was nearly killed, where she and her father's relationship began to distance.

A therapist had once told her that part of her died in those woods that night. Not physically, but somewhere deeper. An emotional, psychological, and likely spiritual part of herself. Amari knew there was truth to the belief. What was worse for her, she thought part of herself died long before then.

Amari entered town from the east end. She drove through the New Hope Arch. An arched entrance at the front of town welcoming visitors. Once on Main Street, she stopped to look up and down the road as she waited for the light to turn. The town looked as she remembered it. The typical historic downtown of many Indiana settlements with tall stone buildings all butted up together. Some retained the original hue of the brick the stone masons had used to build them, while others had been painted. The oldest buildings had layers of paint peeling from random bricks, adding to the figurative crumbling she had experienced there. Though for her—and maybe the buildings, too—it seemed like more than figuratively; it felt literal.

From her position, she noticed there were now stores she had never heard of. Some stores she remembered vividly from her childhood were gone. Only a few had survived the trials of time.

When the light turned, Amari drove again, then noticed one building—where Painted with Love, an art gallery run by Sharon Gilmore had been—sat vacant and appeared to be under reconstruction. Half the building's face had been removed for remodeling.

She could still hear herself laughing with her friends as they had years ago, running down the sidewalks on Friday nights before the game. They would gather their candy from Smitty's, which was now some boutique, then grab a quick dinner at The Shop, which was now closed with no new tenants to replace the beloved eatery.

As much as Amari had changed over the years, so had the town. As she headed out of town from the north, she was happy to see the housing developments or apartment complexes had not encroached yet. She knew it was only a matter of time. Laramy had once told her there would be a time when every inch of land would be filled with concrete. The days of farming would be done in labs or factories. She had laughed at his paranoia, but as she saw the plots of land around her condo rising higher with strip malls, apartments, and housing developments, she wondered if he might not be right.

Lost in her thoughts, Amari didn't realize she had driven past the one-and-a-half-mile driveway on North Markel Road that led her to the cabin. If she kept driving, she would eventually be in another town. Instead, Amari stopped so she could turn around.

# 6

Amari stopped in the road before turning left into the driveway. She was somewhat surprised to find it looked as though the trees and grass at the head of the drive were still maintained. She remembered that in small towns, people regularly went out of their way to care for their neighbors. Even though her father had passed months ago, he had been their neighbor his entire life. She knew even death would not change that. Before his death, her father had told her people from town regularly asked about her. Then, she felt an irrational weight of dread knowing she would likely run into most of them while she was there. Some would even stop by with food, she guessed. She let out a hard sigh before forcing herself to turn down the driveway.

Up until she was ten, Mr. Waters owned the forty acres on which their cabin sat. He would farm the land with either beans or corn, depending on the year, so he could sell them to local markets or restaurants. Two days after her tenth birthday, Mr. Waters had an accident involving a tractor. Her parents never shared the details with her. When Amari never saw him again, she knew what they meant by *accident*. Not long after, her parents let nature reclaim most of the farmland—ten acres of which were left to her parents in Mr. Waters's will. Now the cabin sat behind thick rows of trees. Their yard was about an acre of clear space before the tower of trees claimed the rest.

Amari passed through the seven-foot gap of trees to her yard, where she parked in a small shaded area at the center of the house. The cabin looked the same as she remembered it. The wood of the cabin was a yellow hue, which had always been her favorite color. The front porch ran the length of the structure, the front door at the end of five steps to the left, along two windows, before ending thirty feet from the front door at a porch swing. It was covered by the upper deck, which was open and accessible from the master bedroom. The once-green trim had been painted a deep burgundy, which she did not like. The stone fireplace on the left side of the structure had darkened over the years. She noticed the moss which had begun to grow at the base. The detached garage to the left of the house had been painted to match the house.

As she sat there looking at the house, something in the yard caught her eye. Her attention shifted as she watched.

*Her mother—before the car accident got her hooked on opioids and eventually heroin, before the drugs took their peace as well as Stacy's life—chased after a younger version of Amari. Her mother's jet-black hair floated in the air as if it had a life of its own. Her mother's olive skin seemed to soak up the sun and hold its warmth. The blue summer dress her mother wore made her skin seem more striking. They were laughing as her mother grabbed her from behind. Stacy gently tackled Amari to the ground.*

*Amari's father suddenly popped up from behind a nearby tree. He wore a plaid shirt, unbuttoned to reveal a dirt-stained white tee shirt to accompany his old Levi jeans, the same pair he always wore. He ran to them as fast as he could, then jumped high into the air as if he were going to dogpile on them. Instead, he landed gently just beside them. Amari's mother squawked in faux terror as she covered Amari. Amari put her arms out to catch her father before he lowered himself on top of the two of them, tickling them with the low growling of a wild boar.*

That was a good memory. One of her last good ones. Two years later, her mother was in the accident.

Walking down the country road at dusk to clear her mind, as she did most every night. Usually, Amari would go with her. Not that night, though. On that night, Amari had been mad at her mom. Mad because she would not let Amari spend the night at Katrina Smart's house with all the other girls. Out of disgust—maybe even spite—she told her mother she didn't want to walk with her.

Three hours later, her father was frantic asking where her mom was. That was when Amari began to worry. She had never seen her dad scared before. For the first time in her life, she knew there were things in the world he could not protect her from. As he grabbed his keys to get the truck, there was a heavy knock. Amari answered the door to see Officer Johnson. He told her dad—trying to keep quiet so Amari could not hear, even though she did—that a drunk driver had struck her mom from behind. She had been rushed to the hospital and might have to be airlifted to Bloomington.

Amari's dad rushed them to the hospital, where her mother would stay for almost two weeks. Her left knee had been shattered, her left elbow broken, and her right shoulder dislocated. Months of hospital follow-ups, several surgeries, and physical therapy did little more than start her spiral into addiction from the pain medication.

After the accident, her mother was a different woman. She didn't like to play anymore. She didn't go with Amari and her dad into town. She would spend all her time at home. Amari couldn't remember seeing her mother smile after the accident. Once the doctors started cracking down on prescription opioids, she remembered her mother leaving for a few weeks. Of course, no one told her where she had gone. Amari figured it out later like she usually had to. When her mother came back, things were different for a while. But not very long. Eventually, the broken woman that Stacy had become returned, Amari thought, worse than before.

Amari would be having a conversation with her mom, then, in mid-sentence, her mom would fall asleep. Sometimes when she talked, the words made no sense. There were dark rings all around the crease of her elbow. Her olive skin made the scaring look even darker, which also made them more noticeable to those in town. Amari could hear her parents fighting most nights. The nights they did not fight were the nights her mom would be gone.

Then during Amari's Junior year of high school, she came home from school to find her dad sitting at the kitchen table crying. It petrified her to the point she could have sworn Icy Hot had been injected into her veins. Her muscles felt weak as a distant voice inside her screamed the truth. She knew.

He got up and hugged her in one of his bear hugs. She noticed instantly it felt weaker. Neither of them seemed to have the strength to hold the other, and they collapsed on the floor. He told her, "Mommy is gone."

"Where?" Amari knew the answer. Part of her hoped it would be back to rehab like before. Something was different this time. Her father's tears, mixed with the trembling of his body, told her it was false hope. Her mother would not be back again.

"She was very sick, honey. She tried to stop, but she was just in so much pain…"

"No!" Amari screamed. All the pain and rage boiled over, mixing with the desperation and desolation she felt at the moment. "She was an addict! It was all my fault. If I had been there with her that night, this never would have happened!"

Amari pushed herself away from her father never looking back as she ran out of the house. He called out to her, but she couldn't tell what he was saying.

Later that night, *he* came over. His dark, curly hair bounced on his head, and his sharp cheeks and gentle eyes made her feel comfortable even in the tides of hopelessness. He had found her in the treehouse her father built when she was eight. She had not been up there in years, yet at that time in her life, it was the only place she could think to go.

"What are you doing here?" she asked. Her tears long since dried out, yet the shake in her voice still resonated.

"I heard about your mom," his voice was gentle. He climbed over the edge of the floor and then slid close to her. He put his arm around her. They had been friends since preschool though she had always had a crush on him. They had always only been friends as far as he was concerned. A friend was what she wanted most right then, so she was fine with the arrangement.

She did not bother asking how he had heard. She knew how quickly word traveled through a small town. "It's not fair."

"Life never is," he told her pulling her closer to him. She let herself slide between his arm and body. "I am so sorry you have to go through this."

"I want to leave this stupid town," she said with a deep inhale. She felt her anger returning to take over where the despair had been. "I just want to grab everything I need so I can go somewhere else. Anywhere other than here."

"What about your dad? What about school?"

Then, she could not have cared less about school. In fact, she dreaded it. When she went back, she knew she would have the sympathetic eyes of every student and teacher washing over her. Feeling sorry for the girl whose mom OD'd on heroine. Those who did not have compassion, like Katrina Smart, who stopped talking to her in ninth grade because she missed the sleepover, would mock her. But she couldn't leave her dad. She was all he had.

"We will graduate next year. Then you'll go off to college. Then you can leave this town and everyone in it and do something amazing in the world."

She turned her eyes up at him. "I don't think I want to leave *everyone*."

He smiled down at her and hugged her again. They spent the rest of the night in silence. For the first time in her life, she thought she had an idea of what love felt like. What it was like to be cared for by someone other than family. To care for someone else. When her entire world crumbled around her, the moment she first doubted the fairness of the world and doubted there was a God, when she had recognized the coldness and depravity in the world, she found someone she could trust. Someone who cared about her. Someone who would sneak out in the middle of the night just to check on her. She never dreamed that person would prove her wrong. That it would be him to show her just how dark and merciless the world truly was.

Amari returned from the thought, realizing she was crying. Her eyes were still on the rotten wood of the old treehouse when her thoughts returned to the present. She brought her hand up to rub her eyes. She wished she had never come back home. There was nothing here for her anymore, hadn't been for a long time. She had no real reason to return home.

But then, she wondered if she had come back to prove herself wrong. To show herself she was not weak after all. She could face this. Maybe the world was not as bleak as she believed. Maybe if she could get through this process, she could find healing. Maybe she did not have to live the rest of her life as cynically as she had been. Maybe if she could do that, she would not feel like the past twenty years had all been a façade.

# 7

Amari had taken two trips to unpack her car, leaving the two large duffle bags at the front door. Just by stepping foot in the house, she could tell it had changed a lot since she left after graduation. When her father had moved out, he rented the cabin to vacationers visiting the state park or covered bridges. Eventually, he used apps to book the cabin, and as the boutiques and wineries began popping up around town, he had said it was nearly always reserved. He would stay in the cabin a few weeks each year to hunt or fish. To Amari, it seemed like less than a home, with all the coziness of a weekend getaway. To her, it still felt suffocating.

The house had become little more than a replica of some *Better Homes and Gardens Magazine* cover, with each tacky picture and word sign her father added over the years. Every piece of furniture was a loud white with a yellow plaid design. The carpeting had been ripped up to be replaced with a light linoleum resembling wood flooring. The walls had been painted in a light blue almost too bright for her eyes to handle. Every bulb seemed to be an Edison-style bulb which did not blend well with the light blue paint because it cast an offensive yellow hue throughout their immediate reach turning parts of the wall a ghastly green color.

Fake flowers were on several countertops. The kitchen had been remodeled to host a stainless fridge better suited for a luxury condo than a cabin retreat. The gas lines had been removed so an electric stove top with a double oven could be put in. He had added an island to the kitchen with a granite top. The wall separating the kitchen from the living room had been removed to make the space feel more open. A five-person farm table was all that separated them. There was a 65" television hanging near the fireplace. She was relieved to see it appeared as though it was still wood-burning rather than having been converted to gas.

The spare bedroom downstairs had been converted to a game room complete with a half-sized pool table and a loveseat in front of a 30" television with some gaming system connected to it.

The upstairs was still carpeted, though clearly newer. She guessed it was a year or less old by the plushness and lack of wear in high-traveled areas. Her old room upstairs was a standard bedroom though she did not stay to examine it any further. She did not want to drift off in thought again. She went into the master bedroom, noting aside from a big television and new bedding, the room looked a lot like it did when she was growing up. The door leading to the upstairs balcony had been replaced by glass French doors, which she did not notice when she first arrived. Lightweight curtains covered them to offer privacy when desired yet still allowed the occupant to have an unobstructed view of the woods.

As she stood in the master bedroom, she began running through a mental checklist of what she was going to have to accomplish while at the house. She was planning to sell all the furniture, and perhaps donate the linens to a shelter. Maybe she could sell the appliances? Or if she kept them there, it may be more enticing to a buyer if…

A sharp knock from the front door ripped her from the checklist. She put her hand on her hip to rest the butt of her hand on the grip of her pistol. She felt her heart skip when she didn't feel it. She had left it in the car.

"Dammit!"

Amari descended the steps trying to catch sight of who would be at her door. To her displeasure, none of the windows offered her a clear sight. Even the crescent window atop the door was useless. She reached the door just as another round of knocks came.

She put her right foot on the back of the door as she unlocked it. She opened it just enough to peer around the back of the door to face her visitor.

"Welcome home." The man's voice was familiar. She tried to recall it. Despite her efforts, she could not place it. His brown eyes, auburn hair, and field-tanned skin also seemed familiar. His athletic build and strong stature, however, did not.

"Excuse me?"

"You don't remember me?" His tone sounded as if he were offended. The smile he boasted made Amari question that. She squinted her eyes as if doing so would allow her to see the man before her as he may have looked twenty years before.

"I can't say I do. Sorry."

"Andrew. Andrew Mathis."

Amari felt her jaw drop hard. Her eyes widened in recognition. She forced herself to fix her face to not offend him. She swung the door open, embracing him in a tight hug. It was tighter than she had expected, but he didn't seem to mind.

"Oh. My. God," she pulled herself back to look him over once more. "You've changed so much." In high school, the two had been friends. It was a relationship that had started during their time as lab partners during sophomore year chemistry. They would spend hours together talking about books, science, and the mystical questions of the world. It had been well before her world crumbled beneath her.

"I would have never recognized you!"

Andrew laughed. "In college, I was introduced to the university gym, and having to walk everywhere. I also discovered contacts were a thing."

"You look amazing!"

"Thank you," he beamed. "So do you." Something in how he said his words made Amari smile.

"Jesus, I'm so rude. Come in," she shifted her body to allow him access to the house.

# 8

Amari dug through the kitchen cupboards for two minutes, searching for a pot to boil water in and tea bags or the instant coffee jars her father had always seemed to collect when she was growing up. Andrew came up from behind her, reaching to the top cupboard where they had kept the dishes.

He removed a bag of coffee in his right hand and a French press in his left.

"How did you know where it was?"

"Your dad hired me to do all the maintenance on the place. I also take care of the yard." He handed her the items, then bent down to retrieve an electric kettle from one of the lower cabinets.

"That is what you do full-time?" she asked as he filled the kettle. She plugged it in awkwardly, working around him.

He nodded. "Kind of. I run a construction company. We also do a lot of remodeling. He had a lot of work he wanted done when he started getting more renters. The yard was just a bonus."

"He never told me he hired you."

The light on the kettle clicked off. Andrew poured water into the French press as Amari watched, taking a mental note of how it worked. At times, her life seemed run by either Starbucks drive-thru lines or day-old coffee at the office. She was looking forward to home-brewed coffee for a change.

"Probably figured it wasn't something you'd care about either way. He said you didn't like talking about home much."

Amari accepted a cup he handed her with a shrug. She knew it was true, yet for some reason felt strange admitting it to him.

"He said you're a cop?"

"Was," she corrected him. "For a few years. Now I'm a partner in a private security firm."

"Wow," his face electrified with surprise. "Like a mercenary?"

Amari laughed, raising a hand as if to apologize for her reaction. "No, nothing like a mercenary. We offer private security for celebrities and politicians who come to town. Occasionally people or law firms will hire us to investigate something—affairs, fraud, things along those lines."

"Certainly sounds like being a cop. Why not just stay on at the police department?"

"Better hours," she told him honestly. "I thought if I wanted to have a family or any kind of a personal life at some point, I should probably have a job where I could be home more."

"So, how is the family?"

"Well, as it turns out, just because I *can* have normal hours, it doesn't mean I know how to."

Andrew nodded to show his understanding. "I'm not married either. Running a business is almost a twenty-four-hour gig. Always somebody wanting something. We are running a lot of the remodels downtown."

She hadn't missed the fact he casually threw in the detail about him being single. She didn't acknowledge it. "I know what you mean."

He put his cup on the counter folding his arms, looking around the house with admiration, like an artist who steps back from his painting, pleased with the outcome.

"What's your plan for the place?"

Amari took a deep breath and shook her head. "I honestly don't know. I figured I would start by selling the small stuff. Maybe redecorate so it looks more like a home instead of so much a rental…"

"Hey! I helped decorate this place!" Andrew swiped at Amari's shoulder playfully.

"No offense intended," her smile matched his. She could feel her tension releasing the more she talked with him. "Anyway, after that, I may sell the furniture, then when I get back home, look for a real estate agent to get the place on the market."

"Well, I would be more than happy to help with all of it. I have some contacts. Plus, I imagine it might get tricky if you try to do the whole thing yourself."

"Oh, no," she insisted. "I know you're busy. You said so yourself. I couldn't ask you to do that."

"It's no trouble. I reframed, rewired, and replumbed this whole house. It is my piéce de resistance."

"Do you know how bad your French accent is?" she winked at him.

"Pretty darn good, what about it?"

Amari smiled, "are you sure it wouldn't be too much of a bother?"

"I'm sure. It'll be a nice break. Besides, I can always buy some of the furniture to use in other jobs. Saves you time and energy trying to sell it, plus I get some new inventory."

"Talk about having my cake and eating it, too."

Andrew gave a broad smile. He leaned in to hug her. It felt better than Amari had expected. "I have to get running. I will be by later so we can talk about where you want to get started. It was great seeing you."

"You too," she told him following him to the front door. As he took his final step out the door, she closed it twisting the deadbolt as soon as the latch clicked. She looked around again. Suddenly, it didn't feel so overwhelming.

When she returned to the kitchen, she retrieved a pad of paper and a pen from her purse. She decided to make a series of lists. The first list would be her priorities of things to do—grocery shopping, figuring out what to sell, look for real estate agents. The second list was for her groceries, which included directions to find something nice to cook for Andrew that evening for his kindness and willingness to help with the process. Her last list would be the list of things she wanted to do to the home to make the cabin feel more welcoming for a family willing to make it their forever home. This, of course, led to a new shopping list for supplies.

As each page filled with a new list, the thought didn't escape her that if anyone saw her writing so feverishly, they would comment like every other person who had ever bore witness to the process. *OCD much? You're so extra! Slow down, don't worry about too much at once. You'll burn out.*

What none of those commenters had come to realize was the lists were one of the few things Amari had complete control over. Her life had lacked so much control, and for most of it, she was simply along for the ride. Everything Amari did was a reaction. Rarely had she felt in control of anything. Lists not only gave her control, it also offered a sense of preparedness. If she had a list, she knew what to do, what needed to still be done, but most importantly, a reasonable expectation of the outcome. Without her lists, there would only be anarchy. Amari had experienced enough chaos for two lifetimes.

Amari closed her notepad and then slid it back into her purse. She gave the area one last look. This time, she saw it as it had been the day she left for college, not as it was at that moment. She was back. Home unsweet home.

# 9

Amari realized she felt calmer after seeing Andrew—dare she think relaxed. It was nice having at least one ally in town. Not that she felt anyone in town would be out to get her, but knowing she had someone she could call on since she could not call on her father was comforting. She knew she could always call Laramy, except by the time he arrived, she would already be through whatever crisis arose.

She gathered her shopping list while doing a quick Google search for the nearest grocery store. She had noticed, driving through town, that Strawman's Meat was no longer at the end of the main road. Amari could recall many memories of her and her friends going to Strawman's after school, where Tyler Winston would slide them sticks of bubblegum, sometimes even sliding quarters for the pinball machine, while his dad Benny was not looking. She always assumed Tyler was just being nice to the local kids, then as she got older, figured Benny Strawman probably didn't mind if his son gave freebies to the kids. Benny always lit up when kids filled his store, even when the older men in town would get frustrated by the additional noise disrupting their afternoon coffee circles or preventing them from paying for their groceries and going home because Tyler would be busy listening to the kids tell him about their day.

Tyler had some sort of disability. She could never recall the exact medical term. But Benny never treated his adopted son differently. He spoke to Tyler like an adult, even allowing him the same responsibilities and tasks he would give to any other employee. Amari found herself there wondering what had happened to the family since the store had closed. Then faces of people she grew up with, people she had not thought about in nearly two decades began popping up in her mind. She found herself equally curious about what had become of them. Had they stayed? Had they left? Had they folded their businesses and been forced to work for the other companies which had moved in?

Amari shook the thought away, forcing the list into her back pocket. She returned to her phone to find three stores. All of which were at least a twenty-minute drive out of town. The discount store northeast of town was cash-only. She wondered how they could manage to stay in business. She hadn't carried cash in years, nor could she think of anyone who did. The one southeast would be closing soon after she would arrive, so she chose the furthest store. Thirty minutes southwest. Again, she found herself wondering what had happened to the Strawmans.

When Amari parked at the grocery store thirty minutes later, she felt agitation rising at the sight of a full lot. Acknowledging the new understanding she had of the old men who would groan at her and her friends as kids for holding up the line. It was a thought that made her wince.

Once inside the store, she brought the list from her pocket for review. She began weaving back and forth through the store, methodically adding items from her list to the cart, lost in her concentration on the task at hand. The store was laid out like most supermarkets allowing her to mark items off the list quickly. Except, she didn't notice the man staring at her until he began to approach her. Out of instinct, Amari wrapped her hand tighter around the pen, prepared to strike if she had to. Her eyes landing square on the man approaching from her peripheral.

Amari did not recognize him, but the bright smile behind the graying beard told Amari he recognized her. His green eyes reminded her of someone. She just could not place the rest of his face. The way he walked, with purpose, with command, also felt familiar somehow. She felt her grip on the pen loosen unexpectedly. She waited for him to speak when he reached her.

"Amari Richards?" His voice was calming, instantly making her feel at ease though she didn't understand why. Her guard fell, and the edge which had wrapped around her began to ease.

"Yes. Do I know you?"

The man smiled, his head bobbing from left to right, up and down, in an almost circular motion. "You do. I would not expect you to remember me, though. We only spoke twice. I'm John Meadowbrook."

Amari's eyes widened with part recognition, part shock. The man suddenly appeared twenty years younger. As he stood before her, she guessed he was only in his early to mid-forties, but that night on the road she would have sworn he was the same age back then. The white patches of hair in his beard reflected in the lights as he talked to her in the bed of his truck.

"Ohmygod," the words came out as a single phrase. "I am so sorry."

He raised a hand, "I don't blame you. With what happened to you that night, I was the last thing on your mind. I don't think anyone could remember every detail about something as awful as what you went through."

Amari didn't correct him, but he was wrong. She did remember every dreadful detail. Every smell, every sound, every sight, and every agonizing breath were seared into her memory.

"For some reason, I always thought you were older…" She tried to correct herself but knew it didn't sound any better. "Back then, I mean." She felt her cheeks brighten as blood promptly filled them. "I am sorry, I didn't mean for it to sound so bad."

John laughed. "I was twenty-four then. My father blessed me with some good traits and a lot of good qualities. The early onset of grays was not one of 'em."

"How have you been? I thought about calling a few times. I never could think of how I could possibly express how much I appreciated you stopping for me."

"I don't need no thanks, ma'am. I was just happy to have been there to help. Besides," he said with a warm smile that, in some ways, reminded her of her father's. "I heard through the grapevine you did good for yourself. You've dedicated your career to helping others. Makes it worth everything."

Amari felt herself stiffen. She had never admitted it out loud. Part of her knew she chose her line of work not to help others but instead to help herself. She wanted to feel in control. Mostly she wanted to feel safe. While her line of work came with an inherent danger, at least she was trained. She also always had an entire department of officers behind her. She would never find herself feeling as helpless or alone as she did in those woods.

"What brought you back to town after all this time? Your old man said you didn't like coming back. Understandably."

Amari felt an unexpected lump in her throat, followed sharply by a burn in her eyes. It was a reaction she hadn't anticipated nor planned for, which made her feel more uneasy. "He passed away a few months ago. I'm here to get the cabin ready to sell."

The shame on John's face added weight to her already heavy stomach. Amari realized she felt guilty for some reason. As if she were responsible for his reaction. She felt guilty because of what he had done for her.

"I am so sorry," he said. "I had no idea. I was out of town visitin' my kids out there in California. I can't believe I didn't hear about it. He was a good man."

"Thank you. He surely was."

John's mind seemed to fade into a thought. It was as if part of him had left the store entirely as a memory or an idea played out in his mind consuming his entire focus with whatever images rolled out.

"Well, it was so nice to see you, John."

John returned from the thought with another smile. "You, too," he told her. As Amari turned to continue down her list, he spoke again. "I still go there sometimes. Thinking I can figure out whatever happened to him. I never can, though."

Amari did not turn back to him. She knew if she did, he would see the look in her eyes. The sense of guilt mixed with shame would return. Probably for both of them. "As far as I'm concerned, he died in the river. It swept him off somewhere they could never find him." Even though she knew she didn't believe her words, she hoped he would.

"That would be justice." She heard his cart begin to roll across the tile floor; the sound began to fade after a few seconds. The uncomfortable lump returned to her throat, pushing in all directions threatening to suffocate her. She swallowed hard, trying to force it to disappear. Finally, it cleared as she gripped the handle of the cart to slow the shaking in her hands. She grabbed her list before continuing down the aisle.

# 10

Andrew called Amari on her drive home from the store. He said he would be there around 7 p.m. When she got home, she checked her phone and saw it was already noon. She made a mental note of her goals to complete over the rest of the afternoon. She needed to start looking up donation centers, women's shelters, and a Goodwill to donate the furniture. She took snapshots of some of the larger pieces of furniture along with the artwork so she could post them to various online markets. When she looked at her phone again, it was three. Amari had noticed herself draining; now she could feel herself nearing empty. She had not eaten or stopped for a break since she woke up. Simply walking from one room to the next felt like running a marathon at this point.

Amari found the corner section of the couch in the living room. She tore at the wrapping of a protein bar as she laid back on the plush cushions, which began enveloping her as ravenously as she consumed the bar. She could feel her eyes struggling to stay open. "A short nap might do me some good," she convinced herself.

Amari awoke from her nap on the couch at 5:30. She shot up from the plush cushion with an athletic fluidity she forgot she possessed. She began scanning the house frantically for a clock, finding relief when she saw she had not slept through her dinner with Andrew. She was creating a list in her mind of what needed to be done before he arrived as she made her way up to the master bedroom. Showering, changing, prepping, of course, cooking the meal, but first finding the cookware and dishes. Her mind once again raced without direction. With each item she added to her mental list, two more things followed.

She forced herself to take a deep breath, narrowing her concentration on the first couple of tasks: *getting cleaned up and presentable.*

Amari checked her phone at 6 p.m. She had showered. She found a decent outfit to wear—a pair of khaki shorts coupled with a yellow tank top. She braided her hair and then twisted it into a bun, which she always did when she had to cook. Keeping the hair out of her face allowed her to focus on her task without having to brush hairs away every few seconds.

She found the cookware, silverware, and plates quickly placing them on the table. She diced up peppers before seasoning the roast she had bought with the recommendations of the butcher. The man stood six feet five inches though it had been his strong build which told her the man was well-fueled. He also worked with meat for a living. She figured he knew more about seasoning a roast than any online recipe could even dream of knowing.

She followed his instructions before she slid the roast—which she had surrounded with the peppers tossed with some small potatoes—into the preheated oven and set an alarm for an hour. Already, she could feel sweat beading around her neck and forehead. She looked out the window to the field her dad had helped farm for most of her childhood. Now it was nothing more than an open expanse of grass with small trees trying to claim their place in the world.

A few seconds later, her thoughts were interrupted by the beeping of the timer. Amari looked at the clock as if to question its legitimacy. She had been staring out the window for an hour. Again, Amari had lost time. She knew this had happened a few times since she had returned, but this time was different. This time she was not daydreaming or getting lost in a memory. The time had just passed. That scared her, though now she had no time to torture herself over it.

She removed the roast to let it rest on the stovetop when the ringing of the doorbell bounced through downstairs.

"Come in," she shouted out. She grabbed the knife from the block which rested just in front of her on the counter. Her hand gripped it tightly until she heard Andrew enter the kitchen.

"It smells incredible," he said, taking a whiff. Her grip loosened as she sat the knife down beside the pan.

She turned to him. "It's my specialty."

"Oh, you have a specialty?"

"No, not really. My specialty usually comes from a drive-thru or a soup can." She looked Andrew over suspiciously, then said, "You don't look like a man who just came from a construction job."

Andrew checked his appearance with a broad smile. His t-shirt was spotless, completely devoid of wrinkles. Even his jeans looked as though they had come straight from the dryer. "I showered and changed first. I didn't want to ruin your chances of selling this place by stinking it up."

"I appreciate it." Amari turned to the fridge retrieving two bottles of Coors. She sat one down in front of her on the island, sliding the other to where Andrew was walking.

"I actually don't drink," he told her. The way his words came felt like he was ashamed of them. The way his eyes followed the bottle as she pulled it back also held a story.

"I have Diet Coke or water," she offered.

"I'll take a Diet Coke."

"So, do you just not like beer, or is there another reason you don't drink?" She had tried to make the question sound innocent, but even as the words crossed her ears, she felt there was a hint of accusation.

"I used to drink a lot. Too much. Way too much, if I'm to be honest. About two years after you left, I was coming home from work when I blew a stop sign and plowed into a parked car."

Amari said nothing, letting him talk and allowing herself to absorb his words. His pain was familiar to her.

"Fortunately, no one was in the car. Thank God. I still spent a month in jail and lost my license for a little bit. It really woke me up."

"It is amazing you woke up at all. Some people never learn from their mistakes. They just keep chasing the same demons."

"Or running from them," he pointed out.

Amari felt her face redden. She slid the beer away, turning to the roast so she could begin slicing it. She heard Andrew's chair slide away from the island followed by his footsteps closing in on her. She felt his presence beside her.

"I didn't mean for it to sound like that. I wasn't talking about you. I just meant that some people spend their whole lives running from something they will never face. You did. I mean, you face scary things every single day."

Amari blinked a tear away. "No, you're probably right. I ran from this place." She put the food on the plates trying to refocus her mind, shaking her head in disgrace. "I became a cop because I thought it would allow me to protect others from ever feeling what I did. Truthfully, I did it because it was the ultimate form of self-preservation. It was just another way I could run."

"You came back. That takes real courage."

Amari wiped her eyes with her forearm before she gave Andrew his plate. "Let's eat. Maybe talk about something less touchy."

Andrew smiled. "Fair enough."

The two ate mostly in silence. Then once the plates were cleared and a conversation sparked, they became lost in the stories of how their lives unfolded over the twenty years that separated their memories of each other. The losses, along with the gained pearls of wisdom, the embarrassments, as well as the successes. Time passed without their realization. For the first time in recent memory, Amari was content. She forgot about the darkness wandering the crests of the earth—more importantly, the darkness that had occupied the distant parts of her mind.

"You know," Andrew said, "I think part of what makes you so good at your job is the fact you were trying to distance yourself as much as possible from the whole situation. The deeper you got into policing and the tougher you became, the less victim you could be."

Amari took a sip from her water to hide her discomfort. She forced a smile. "I thought serious topics were off limits?"

Andrew raised his hands in concession. As he brought them back down, the motion lights at the rear of the house went off. Without pause, Amari stood from her seat. Without hesitation, she went to her purse on the couch behind Andrew, retrieving her 9mm pistol and gripping it with intent.

"What are you doing?" Andrew asked falling in behind her as Amari twisted the lock of the back door and stormed outside.

Amari raised the gun so she was staring down the sights sweeping left to right. To the right of the house, just below the motion lights, a raccoon sat on the top of a trashcan observing them questioningly. It appeared almost frustrated at Amari for rudely barging in on its dinner.

"A raccoon," Andrew snickered. "I told you so."

Amari turned mischievously, smacking Andrew's arm.

Andrew played the role of an injured bystander. "Oh! What did I do?"

Amari smirked, "You never tell a woman, 'I told you so.'"

Andrew smiled with a surrendering nod. "Point taken. It was great catching up. And dinner was delightful. Thank you."

"Anytime. Thank you for the company."

Andrew leaned in, embracing Amari with a gentle hug. "I will see you in the morning?"

"Yes. I will be ready to work."

"Good," he smirked. Andrew spun on the heels of his feet, walking through the backyard to round the house.

Amari stood there alone in the dark turning her focus to the woods. Part of her felt uneasy, feeling invisible eyes caressing her, tracking her every breath, trying to anticipate her next move. Like a lion stalking down on its prey. A shiver shot through her core as she wrapped her arms around herself. The raccoon seemed to laugh. She glared at the furry bandit. As the unease continued to grow, she decided to go back inside. Once the door was closed, she locked it before pulling the cord for the blinds. She went into the blackness of the living room, where the eyes could no longer follow her.

# 11

For hours, Amari tried diverting her mind away from the unwavering thought someone was watching from the darkness of the tree line. She had mindlessly scrolled the same movie selection on her television for three hours until she felt her eyes grow heavy. The burn of sleepiness tugged at her eyelids. Leaving the television on for the extra light, Amari grabbed the gun from the cushion beside her and then made her way up the stairs to her room.

Once in her bedroom, she walked over to the French doors of the balcony. She checked the locks twice. While she doubted a person would be able to scale the house to the balcony, she was not willing to take a chance. Amari placed her gun on the nightstand resting on her side of the bed. She disrobed, then changed into a pair of pajama bottoms and the IU sweatshirt she received during freshman orientation. It had been stained and worn to near threads, but still she refused to let it go. A therapist had once told her, "Seems to be a pattern in your life." It had been the last time Amari went to see her, even though she often returned to those words knowing there was truth in them.

Once she was dressed, she checked the doors one more time before lying down. Her father had not skimped on the mattress. It felt like a memory foam that wrapped itself around her, cradling her like a gentle cloud which nearly sucked the last bit of consciousness away from her.

Before rest could take hold, she jolted back to life. She heard something downstairs. She couldn't place it at first so she turned her ear toward the door. Amari held her breath until she heard it again. It sounded like a window sliding up its frame.

Amari reached for her gun on the counter beside her, rising gently from the bed to avoid causing the floors to squeak. She crept toward the door on the balls of her feet, each step calculated so she would not betray her movements. She grabbed the handle, still listening for any noise that may have been able to alert her to the exact source of the sound. She twisted the knob slowly to be sure the latch could not click. Amari pulled at the door, sliding her body through the small opening she had created. She poked her head through just enough to see the hall was clear. Once satisfied she was at least alone upstairs, she slid the rest of the way out into the hall.

Amari raised the gun up to her chest as she leaned over the banister with the gun pointing down. The light from the television bled into the hall from the living room. She could not see any shadows. Worse, she did not hear any more movement. She stood there a moment longer, listening intently.

She reversed her step until her back just touched the wall at the top of the steps. She kept her eyes over the banister as she descended one step at a time, her finger just outside of the trigger guard but the gun pointing outward, ready to strike. At the bottom of the steps, she brought the gun up directly ahead of her, allowing her to move tactfully toward the kitchen. Amari pressed her back to the wall where the corridor entered the kitchen and living room. She leaned slightly right to get a look into the living room, which was empty. Amari twisted her body so she could lean against the opposite wall, then did the same thing for the kitchen. Satisfied both rooms were empty, she checked the windows to ensure they were still locked. Amari went through each of the downstairs rooms.

Even though Amari was sure the house was empty, she turned on all the lights, feeling ridiculous for her overreaction. She knew she heard something. She was not imagining that. Amari went to the kitchen. She pulled her cell phone from her purse, where she opened her internet browser. She typed quickly, then once she found what she was looking for, she pressed the phone icon, which dialed the local Sheriff's Department.

When the two deputies arrived fifteen minutes later, they also cleared the house in a similar methodical fashion to Amari. The main difference was the two men had been so certain the house would be empty that neither drew their weapon. The taller of the two men, who showcased a thick and wild beard perfectly paired with a crew-cut hairstyle, came down the stairs. The shorter man with deep dark skin and doubtful eyes sunken into his clean-shaven face came from the downstairs hall.

They whispered to each other for a while inside before they met Amari on the porch.

"The house is clear, Ma'am," the taller deputy said. Amari looked at his name badge. Martinez.

"We checked each room as well as every window. Everything was locked and secure." She checked his name as well. Williams.

"Thank you both. I guess I'm a little on edge."

"You've been away from the woods too long," Martinez said.

"Excuse me?"

"Your family owned this cabin, right? You grew up here then left for college?"

Amari didn't bother asking how he could be so certain. Even though neither of these men had lived there when Amari was attacked, she knew how gossip worked in small towns. "Yes, correct."

"There's a lot of animals that come around to dig through trash. Dig through gardens. Probably just a raccoon or squirrel running along a window sill."

Amari felt a crushing sense of foolishness as her mind went back to the raccoon she and Andrew had caught in the backyard setting off the motion lights.

*What the hell is happening to me,* Amari thought. "Thank you, officers. I'm sorry for wasting your time."

"Not a waste at all, Ma'am," Williams smiled comfortingly. She couldn't tell if it was genuine or a coached response. "It's always better to be safe than sorry. Especially if you are out here alone."

"What is that supposed to mean?" Both officers tensed at her resentment.

"Just—if you're alone, there's no one to call backup," Williams clarified.

"I can't deny you make a good point."

Amari shook their hands taking a business card from Williams who promised she could call any time and he would be there to assist her. She was not sure if he was flirting with her or not. Either way, she had no interest in trying to test the dating waters there. Nothing in the world would keep her in town longer than she had to be there. As soon she finished figuring out how to deal with the house and the furniture, she would be gone. Once and for all, she would be done with the town.

# 12

Amari's eyes fluttered open at 6 a.m. She felt unsure if she had fallen asleep at all. After the officers left, she spent the next two hours lying in bed, listening intently for any noise she thought sounded the least bit out of place. The last time she remembered checking her phone, it was a little after three in the morning. She lay there, wanting to just close her eyes so she could sleep for a few more hours, but knew Andrew would be there before too long, expecting to work. She would be of little use to him if she was fighting sleep. She needed coffee, preferably in the form of an intravenous line.

Amari moved as though through sludge. She made her way down the steps. Each step felt as though her body could only move in slow motion, yet her brain felt weightless. It had been a long time since she had to function off three hours of sleep. At the security firm, she would either sleep all day after an all-nighter or not sleep at all, just ride the waves. Against her own logic, three hours of sleep felt worse than either of the other options.

Once downstairs, she went straight to the French press cursing it twice as she tried to remember how Andrew had worked it. Once she disassembled it to put the coffee in, she started the water to boil, then retrieved a bagel from the counter alongside a banana. She was going to need the caffeine tag teaming the sugar rush. She just hoped when the crash came, she would be occupied with other tasks to help keep her moving.

Amari poured her coffee into a cup tilting back two sips and sandwiching a bite from her bagel between them.

Suddenly feeling less like a zombie and more like a living creature. Not quite human, but at least functional.

A squared sheet of paper on the kitchen table caught her attention. She replayed the night before in her mind. Even through her exhaustion, she was nearly certain Andrew had not left anything. Amari was positive she had not left anything. It was too big to be the business card Deputy Williams had handed her. She wondered if maybe he had written his information down and left it on the table. Maybe he had been flirting after all. The idea made her nauseous. It was a grave misuse of power. No officer should be flirting with the scared woman they were dispatched to, certainly not when they are clearly uninterested.

Amari felt the heat of frustration rise inside her. It mixed with a sense of disgust and a hint of disappointment in the fellow officer. She put her cup and bagel down on the counter harder than she had meant to, especially since there was no one present for the show.

She stormed to the table, ready to read the note Williams had left her, already planning the complaint she would call to file once her suspicion was confirmed. As she read the words, her anger and frustration began to give way to terror, which caused her hands to tremble. She closed her eyes so tightly they ached. Amari opened them to make sure the words were real.

*Welcome home. I've been waiting.*

She flipped the squared sheet over to search the back. Only those five words were written. They stayed there, mocking her. Taunting her. She dropped the page, barely noticing her knees weakening, threatening to collapse under her weight. She grabbed the top of the table when the faintness became overpowering. It was the only thing preventing her from falling. Her attention went to the window near the sink, where she scanned what little of the tree line she could see. She took a deep breath to steady her heart rate. Relatively sure she would not collapse, she raced for the stairs. She rose the steps two at a time. Once her Smith & Wesson was tightly gripped in her hand, she felt her heart rate slow a little more, no longer threatening to burst through her chest.

Amari went back downstairs, where she walked out of the back door almost on auto-pilot. She had no control over her movements. They were reactionary, not meticulously thought out, planned, and then executed. Which was foreign to her.

*"Stop! Plan your move!"* a voice screamed in her head.

She ignored it until she reached the edge of the tree line. She made her way along the line, looking to the ground for any sign something of substantial weight had trespassed through. Any evidence the brush had been disturbed or broken. She also observed the space just beyond the tree line for anything indicating someone had obviously been sitting there. Watching.

Were they there watching her last night? Was that what she had felt?

Amari could feel her fear transform into a rage, intensifying and replacing the coldness rushing through her veins. It threatened to boil the blood running through them. Her face felt hot. Her neck grew sticky with perspiration. Part of her hoped whoever left the note was still there so she could find them.

At the far end of the tree line, Amari spotted a small gap in the tall grass. It looked like a game trail. She thought a careful human could utilize the trail to travel without disturbing much of anything. Amari pulled the slide of her pistol back just enough to verify the brass in the chamber. She took a cautious step into the woods making sure her bare feet did not find a twig or shards of broken glass.

Amari went only a few feet into the woods, scanning again. Nothing seemed out of place.

Then, without warning or alert, a strong hand laid itself on her shoulder.

Amari spun to face the stranger in the woods, pointing the barrel of her gun straight at the forehead of the man behind her.

"Whoa, what the fuck?!" Andrew ducked down as low as the earth would allow, his hands defensively raised over his head, tucking his face down to the ground.

"Oh, shit!" Amaria laid her gun down on the dirt as she pressed herself to Andrew, her hands on his shoulders. "I'm sorry. I didn't know you were coming so early."

She felt Andrew's body relax just before he turned his face to her lowering his hands. "What the hell is going on?" Amari felt a tsunami of guilt smash into her, threatening to carry her off. She felt like she was losing herself in this place again.

For a moment, she thought about showing Andrew the note. Telling him about hearing the window slide open, which had forced her to call the police the night before. Then she wondered, what would he think of her? Would he think she was crazy? Would he believe her? Would he leave her to face her lunacy alone?

"Amari," he said. The concern in his eyes made the tides of guilt stronger.

"I have to show you something."


Andrew studied the squared sheet for a while before his eyes rose again to meet Amari's. "I don't get it. What am I looking at?"

"I found it on my table this morning. Last night after you left, I felt like someone was watching me from the woods. When I went to bed, I heard something at the window," she pleaded her case as she pointed to the window behind the sink. "I couldn't find anyone in the house, so I called the Sheriff. A couple of deputies didn't see anything either, so whoever left this did it after they went through. He could have been in my house all night, Andrew."

A disbelieving sigh escaped Andrew as if he wanted to comfort her but didn't believe the concern. He stayed silent for a moment as if no words he could think of seemed good enough. Then he spoke with uncertainty, "It was probably just some teenagers."

"Why would teenagers sneak into my house at four in the morning?"

Andrew shook his head, not quite believing the idea himself but not wanting her to know it. "You are kind of an urban legend around here. Kids tell your story to each other. They make dares to go into the woods at night near the river. It's no secret you're back. I'm sure someone jumped at the opportunity to see the woman who survived the attack of Skinner's Woods." Andrew took a step toward Amari. He put a comforting hand on her shoulder and then, in a single motion, pulled her in for a hug.

Amari let herself feel the comfort of his arms for a moment before she pulled herself away. "I don't think kids would be so stupid."

"Have you not been keeping up with the moronic internet challenges?"

Amari shook her head. "It's him. I know it is."

"Who?"

"*Him.*"

"Samael Skinner?" Amari winced at the name. Andrew noticed. He lowered his head in sympathy. Then his eyes rose compassionately. "Amari, he's dead. You know that."

"Do I?" Amari felt her frustration growing. It was the same conversation she had repeatedly with people promising he was dead despite never having anything to show her to prove it. "His body was never found, no clothing was ever found, nothing was ever recovered to suggest he even went into the river."

"He lost a lot of blood. There was a clear trail of it which led to the river. It was so flooded it was moving fast. Plus, he probably had a concussion. He could have gone anywhere."

"Still, no one has found his remains. What if those murders lately are him? What if he has been perfecting his MO? Now, he knows I'm back here; he is going to come after me again."

Andrew took her hand into his. "I can't even imagine what all of this is bringing up inside of you. Even if he didn't get swept off by the river, why start killing now? Why has he not been doing this for the past twenty years? Why come after you now? You believe these things are related because you never got the closure you deserved."

Andrew smiled at her, attempting to lighten the tension. "Besides, if it were Sam, you are a badass. You would handle him just like you did the first time. As I learned, there is no way he would be able to get away again. Besides, I won't let anything happen to you, either. If it will help, I will ask around to see if anyone has heard anything about the kids in town planning stupid pranks."

Amari's tensed muscles relaxed noticeably. The rebar-strength tension formed in her neck softened. "I didn't know you were so sweet," she teased.

Andrew's head came down, so his eyes were lined up with hers. "You just never paid attention."

# 13

Andrew was focused on wrapping up some of the decorative pieces of furniture, while Amari headed up to the attic. Her father had kept most of their possessions—their material memories—stored up there because his failing knees made it hard to climb the attic ladder. The idea of him climbing up and down with boxes had sent Amari into a tirade at the mere mention of the idea. Under protest, he had sworn he would wait until she arrived. She was not sure what was up there exactly. She supposed there were boxes of pictures, boxes from her old room, things of her mother's that her dad had never thrown out. To him, memories were all he had left of his family.

In the attic, Amari flipped the switch wired to the beam directly to the right, flooding the dark room with a burst of stale yellow radiance. The sudden brightness combined with her movements caused decades of dust to flutter through the air. Some found their way to her lungs, sending her into a coughing fit. It reminded her of when she was eight, when she had been diagnosed with Exercise-Induced Bronchoconstriction—which she, fortunately, grew out of when she was sixteen.

The attic had at one time been used as her father's office. He had wired it for electricity and temperature control—though as she stood there with sweat forming on every inch of her flesh, she doubted it still worked. He had even put in flooring. He would go up there sometimes for hours. When he did, she never heard any of the distinct noises she had imagined an office would produce. No papers rustling or keys typing. Just silence. Now as she stood there, she wondered why a farm laborer would need an office. Perhaps it had simply been his polite way of saying he needed his own time.

Her mother had once told her, "It is his little getaway." When Amari heard that, it hurt. As if he were wanting to get away from *her*.

Now the attic showed how forgotten it had become over the decades. The dust floating through the air moments before came to rest on the already-coated floor. Mouse droppings lined the corners of the room. She didn't dare consider how many spiders might lurk in the shadows and crevasses.

Amari rolled up her sleeves as she stepped fully into the open space examining from a distance the dozens of boxes around the room. Her father had the foresight to label them and stack them mostly by category. From where she stood, she could see a stack of boxes labeled *Mom's Stuff*. Another one *Dad's Stuff*. Against the far back wall on top of an old desk, *Mari's Room*. The stack that held her attention was the one to her right, towering in front of the dormer window, blocking the sunlight. It had been labeled, *Family Memories*.

She stared at the boxes for a time shorter than it felt. Though, mostly, time just seemed to stop. The boxes were stacked five tall, just wide enough she was concerned about being able to wrap her arms around them. Amari went to the boxes as if entranced by their presence and without control of her body. She grabbed the top box, shaking it to test its weight, then pulled it down catching the squared box before dropping it to the floor.

Upon opening the box, she was face-to-face with a stack of photos under a hard-cased notebook binding aged yellowed paper. A large brown stain had formed across the top of the red cover. Amari grabbed the notebook and a handful of photos. She placed the photos on the lid before she opened the journal.

The words were scribbled in her father's handwriting. Page after page of descriptions about his day. Things he had been struggling with. Things Amari and her mother did that lit up his world. She read some pages, skimmed others, and then stopped when she reached the last entry. It was two days after she had been attacked, then he never wrote in it again.

*God, I am so thankful, yet so sick! How could my precious little girl have gone through something so terrible? Where was I? Why was I not there to protect her? Jesus, she must've been so scared. I was at the hospital yesterday. All she could do was cry; I tried holding her, tried telling her it would all be okay. I know she is too smart to believe such empty words. She knew nothing would ever be okay. First, she loses her mother. Then she nearly loses her life. I am so grateful she is the strong and courageous woman she is because I have no doubt that is what kept her alive when the monster tried to take her from this world. Still, I cannot stop this guilt I have. It's suffocating. I should have been there.*

Amari remembered the exact night in the hospital.

*Amari was strapped to the bed with tubes running in all directions. The nurses had said something about fluids followed by something regarding pain management. Nothing made sense. A doctor had talked to her about surgery so they could make sure there wasn't any serious damage. How could she possibly be any more damaged than she already was? If she were, how could they conceivably fix what had been broken?*
*She stared off at the ceiling as they spoke, trying to be somewhere else. Anywhere else other than where she was right then. She remembered she had asked for her dad. Someone she did not recognize had said they would call. When had that been? How long had she even been in the*

*hospital? Everything moved so fast at times, then so agonizingly slow at others. Time seemed to be a concept which no longer held meaning to her.*

*She had asked if they had found him. Was Samael alive, or was he dead? No one had any answers. Not even the deputies who questioned her. They just gave her sympathetic glances. They danced around the answer. In the end, it had been the same each time. They believed he fell into the river. They said he had not been located. Something about search parties and dogs. She heard what she needed to, so nothing else mattered.*

*A nurse came in to give her a shot of antibiotics to ensure there would be no infections. She asked again about her dad. Each time the nurse promised he was only two minutes away. She had just spoken to him, she said. Amari could not grasp what two minutes meant. To her, each second was like a never-ending crawl.*

*She started to feel nauseous. The nurse must have noticed something on her face because she had pressed a button. A moment later, the feeling retreated. The nurse talked to her, but the words sounded so far away. It was as if Amari were not truly there at all.*

*Then she saw him coming down the hall, rushing and sweating... or crying? He had come into the room breathless. Her father looked like a man she had never met. Sprouts of gray she had never noticed before had risen from his thick brown hair. It sprawled in every direction as if he had been standing in a tornado yet somehow managed to walk through it. His clothes were wrinkled with patches of mud along the lower quarter of his jeans. His face seemed to have aged five years in only a few hours.*

*The pain in his blue eyes, flooded with the tears that fell from them as he approached her, hurt more than the stab wound. No matter how many times she pushed the button beside her, she knew it would not take it away.*

*Her father had sat beside her, and he took her hands into his. The rough callused flesh felt comforting to her. The scent of her father smelled of safety. At last, she could let go. The tears came hard and fast, which made it a challenge to even breathe.*

*"Oh, Mari. I am so, so, sorry."*

*She couldn't speak through the tears so she squeezed his hand. She wanted to tell him it was what he had told her that kept her alive. It was because of him she had fought so hard. He was there with her, even if he did not know it.*

*"I should have asked you to stay home. I should have paid more attention to the boy." He leaned down, and he wrapped her gently into his arms. "I hope they never find him. Because if they do, I swear to the Lord, I will take his life."*

**"Amari!"**

# 14

Amari returned from the memory with a shout. She spun her head to see Andrew, who faced her with a pallid tone on his typically sun-kissed face. His eye sitting too wide for any human. As the realization set in that it was him she was seeing, she put a hand on her chest.

"Are you okay? What is going on?" Amari was nervous about what he must be thinking. Twice now, she had acted like a nutcase when he had caught her off guard. She knew it was not a normal reaction, not for any typical person.

Somehow Amari could only laugh. "I'm sorry. I didn't hear you come up."

"I was calling for you. I wanted to ask about some of the stuff downstairs."

"I was somewhere else," she told him honestly, turning to put the journal and pictures back into the box. "Can you take this whole stack to my room?"

Andrew crossed the attic the rest of the way so he could test the weight of the box she had been rummaging through. "Yeah, I will go down there if you can slide them down to me."

"I can manage that."

Once the stack was gone from the attic, Andrew began moving them to her room. In the attic, Amari noticed a safe under the sill of the dormer. It had been hidden by the boxes, and even still, with the boxes removed, it was tucked deep into the shadows of the space. She bent down to get a better grip on the sides. It was heavy, though not so heavy she didn't think she couldn't move it alone. She lowered her body as she slid the small safe free from its space. The floor squalled a quick protest under the shifting weight as if the steel container had become as much a part of the house as the floor itself.

When it was free, she lifted it. She was glad to feel it was lighter than she had first thought. For all she knew, it may have been empty. Most of the weight felt well distributed as if the steel container contributed more to the weight than any contents. She set it to the side of the attic entrance. Amari would return to it later. After Andrew had left.

Amari decided she would focus on the clearing of boxes later. Her entire body was now saturated with sweat, the heat was beginning to make her head throb. She looked at the stacks of boxes one more time before descending the ladder.

# 15

This was his favorite part: the hunt. He could always smell their fear in the air. People who knew they were about to die always had the sweetest smell. Sure, the scent was sweet when he started the game. But when they knew they would not win, the aroma was divine. When the fact could no longer be avoided, when all hope had melted away, the scent made him crave it more.

This time was no different. He could smell the girl through the thick heat of the night as she ran into the woods, desperate to escape. He could hear her stumbling in the distance. She had stopped screaming long ago when he caught her the first time. Like always, he let her go. He wanted to enjoy the chase. Had he killed her then, it would be over. He had wanted to save this moment for Amari once he knew she'd returned to New Hope. The hunger and lust for the chase was too strong to wait, but it still was not time for her. He hoped for the time being, this one would satiate the growing hunger in his soul.

As he continued through the woods, he took his time, remaining cautious to not make any noise. She was as foolish as all the rest, running in a straight line through the forest. He wondered why they always did that. Sometimes they would veer off in one direction or another, but even then, they would remain true to their course for the most part until they were forced to change direction again. Either because of him or some other obstacle.

As he headed in her direction, he began to spin the knife blade on his thumb. He thought back to when he knew his current prey would be the one—he wished he knew her name. He had been driving down Main Street when he saw her leave the boutique shop. She must have worked there because she was locking the door when he stopped at the light. She tugged at the door to ensure it had latched, then began walking in the same direction as he was going. As if it were fate.

Her spiraled blond hair with violet flairs danced in the wind. Her innocence was almost as palatable as her fear would be later. She tried hard not to look at him as he drove slowly behind her. She started walking faster. He knew he might lose her if she started running. He could have jumped out of the vehicle, grabbed her, then taken her to the special place. Except, to him, there was no thrill in that. It took away from the game he cherished so much.

Instead, he pulled up beside her, rolling down his window as his vehicle slowed. "I am so sorry to bother you, miss. I'm looking for Barger's Cove and everyone seems to be closed. Do you know where that is?"

She looked at him suspiciously, which made his hunger grow. Her gray eyes held doubt but also just enough trust he thought she might fall for his game. Finally, she stepped forward just a couple of steps. He knew he would not grab her. Not yet. He was too entranced in her eyes and imagining how they would look in the end.

"You go three miles up there," she said, pointing in the direction he was headed. "Take the first left, go two more miles, then just take the second right. There will be signs once you make the first left."

He slapped his forehead as if it were so obvious, he couldn't believe he had missed it. "I took a right the first time. What an idiot."

She forced a laugh as smooth as honey. "No worries." She began walking again.

"Say, it probably isn't all too safe for a young lady to walk alone at night. Do you need a ride?"

"No thanks," she said without looking back. Her pace quickened slightly, but not enough to make it seem as though she saw him as a threat.

"Are you sure?"

"Yes," her voice seemed agitated as her pace picked up more. "My dad is picking me up around the block."

He knew it was a lie. "Okay, have a good night." He pulled away slowly. He knew if he were to just leave it would make her feel secure, as if he were making a genuine offer to assist her and he had no malintent. It almost always worked.

"Hey!" She yelled when he was fifteen yards past her. She ran up to his window. "I guess a ride wouldn't be so bad. You'll be going right by my place anyway."

He gave her a surprised look. "What about your dad? Won't he be expecting you?"

"I can just text him I found a ride. He isn't supposed to be here for another fifteen minutes. I don't really want to wait."

He shrugged as if the comment meant nothing to him, though it meant everything. He unlocked the door and waited for her to round the front to get in. Once she was inside, he sat there silently, watching her. He could tell she was beginning to rethink her decision, so he acted.

Pointing to her seatbelt, "Safety first."

She let out a sigh, letting the tension in her chest escape. "Right, sorry."

Once he heard the click, he drove off. Between giving him directions, they talked about her school before moving on to where she planned to go to college the next year. With each second, she grew more relaxed and more trusting.

Then he drove past where she said to turn. Instead, he sped up. The scent of her fear came on faster than most. Stronger, too. He turned down a dark road he knew would lead right to Skinner's Woods.

"I'm going to stop the car. When I do, you get thirty seconds to go as far as you can. Then the game starts."

"What the fuck are you talking about! Let me out of the car!" She tried to hit him. She didn't know it just made him hungrier.

He stopped the vehicle, flipping the lock. She jumped from the car like they always did. She ran right into the woods. He had wondered once why they never stuck to the road. He supposed the instinct to run in a straight line was a powerful one. They probably assumed they could outrun him in the woods better than they could outrun his car on the road.

He counted to thirty, then got out of the vehicle casually. He followed her screaming for a hundred yards. She didn't stop until he was within thirty feet of her. To his dissatisfaction, he quickly found her behind a boulder. He laughed at her thoughtless attempt as he told her to try again. Thirty seconds later, he was back on the move, taking the knife from his sheath and letting the tip twirl on his thumb.

He found the girl hiding behind a log the second time. She was trembling. He just watched her as she thought she had made it through the game. Like always, he was going to win.

When he was done, he looked at his work in admiration. His hunger was filled. For now. He hoped this hunt would be enough to satiate him until it was time to play it with Amari.

He put the girl's cell phone in his pocket. In an hour, he would park outside of the store she had left, where he would call the police so he could tell them he had killed her and where they could find the body. It was something he had never done before, but he wanted to make sure they would find her. He did not want to waste any time on another nobody.

He knew if the hunger became too strong, he would have to change his plan. He might have no choice other than to start the game early. It would not be the worst thing. Still, it would not be as marvelous as he had always imagined it to be. He had been waiting a long time for that sweet moment. He wanted to enjoy every second of it.

# 16

Amari had just finished pouring her coffee when she heard the knock on the door. She checked the clock above the stove. It was far too early for Andrew to be arriving. She had reached out to some realtors though nothing had been scheduled. She had basic questions she wanted answered, which she knew could be done over the phone. Google had provided far too many varying opinions on how to handle inherited properties, all before the issue of taxes.

Amari grabbed the mug with her left hand before she headed for the front door. Another knock—more impatient and hurried—came booming through the house. It was a familiar knock. The kind of knock she had done more times than she could count. She stuck her eye to the peephole to find two deputies; her suspicions were confirmed.

She opened the door greeting the two officers with a smile. The deputy to her left, Loust, according to his name badge, looked like a true-blue rookie. He was no more than twenty-one or twenty-two, by her best estimate. He had a close-shave hairstyle where his bright blond hair nearly vanished entirely from his head. His skin was still smooth, and the relentless bags that never seemed to leave the eyes of a veteran officer were nowhere to be found.

The officer to Amari's right, Cleary, must have been his training officer. She was Amari's age, perhaps a year or so younger. The woman's jet-black hair sat tied in a bun held high and tight. Obviously, she had done it many times. The bags under Cleary's eyes were visible by a trained observer, though Cleary had done a magnificent job blending over them with her makeup. She seemed harder, as though she had been on patrol since the day she left the academy.

"Good morning, Deputies. I don't think I called again. Did I?"

Cleary smiled, shaking her head. "No, Ma'am. We are here for another reason. May we come in?"

Amari had the most likely scenarios run through her mind. There had only been a few reasons she had asked the same question when she was an officer. She was either arresting someone, informing them of a tragedy, or questioning them regarding an event. She had not broken the law, she had no one else to lose, and lastly, she had not left the cabin to have witnessed anything. The former officer in Amari felt comfortable letting them in.

"Sure," Amari offered another smile. "Can I get either of you some coffee?"

"I would love some," Cleary told her as she walked past Amari, heading straight for the kitchen.

"Yes, thank you, Ma'am." Loust's voice even shared how fresh he was.

She followed the deputies to the kitchen, then directed them to the two bar stools at the island. They smiled politely but did not sit. Amari retrieved two cups and filled them with coffee, before sliding them across the counter to the officers. Once the officers had their coffee, they each took a quick sip, then nodded their approval of the full-bodied dark roast. They both put their cups down on the counter in unison. The smoothness of the synchronization forced Amari to bite her lip to keep from laughing.

"So, what can I do for you, Deputies?"

The two looked at each other with a solemnness Amari didn't like. Had she misread the situation?

"We came here to inform you a young woman was found murdered last night."

Amari's heart stopped. Somehow, her legs held true. She didn't feel like she was breathing, however. She felt her stomach fold in on itself. For a moment, she thought she might vomit.

"Why are you telling me?"

"The Sheriff knows your history. She didn't want you to be alarmed."

"Alarmed? Why would I not be alarmed?! Who was she? What happened?" The questions came out quickly. Amari's mind flashed back to her attack, then back to her conversation with the officers.

"Melissa Height. She was a seventeen-year-old senior walking home from work. She was picked up somewhere between the boutique she worked at and home about three miles from there. She was stabbed multiple times. Her body was left in Skinner's Woods." Cleary tried to give the details as if they were simple facts. To Amari, they were anything but.

"A seventeen-year-old female is killed in Skinner's Woods, yet you don't think that is something I would find at all concerning? It is a mirror image of what the fuck nearly happened to me!" Amari's body folded. She had to catch herself on the counter. "It's him, isn't it?"

"We don't know who it was, Ma'am," Loust told her. His voice shaking.

"State Police think it is the same guy who has been committing the murders up and down I-65."

Amari's eyes rolled. "Of course, they do. What do you think?"

"We think it is unrelated. Maybe a copycat."

Amari looked to Cleary, who seemed to do most of the talking and to hold most of the details. "Why do you think that?"

Amari could tell Cleary was weighing the risks of divulging any information to someone outside of the Sheriff's office. What consequences may come from revealing even the slightest detail? Then, she made her decision. "I should not really divulge any information related to an open investigation."

Amari looked at her and appealed with desperation. "Cop to cop, woman to woman, I need to know."

Cleary looked over to Loust, and they had a short conversation with their eyes. Amari imagined Cleary was telling him that *sometimes you need to use judgment on what and to whom you reveal information.* Then Cleary returned her attention to Amari.

"The suspect used Melissa's cellphone to report the murder, in addition to where to find the body. It's not something the other guy does."

"Unless he wanted to make sure you would find it."

"Why would he want to do that?"

Amari gave Cleary a look, conveying her surprise Cleary didn't see the obvious. As if it were the only logical conclusion anyone could come to. "Because he knows I'm here. He wants me to know he is too."

Cleary and Loust exchanged a puzzled look, seemingly confused by Amari's statement. She imagined the conversation was either a silent accusation of her being delusional or they were completely unaware of the person she was referring to.

"Who are you talking about?" Loust had been chosen to be the one to ask the question. Amari guessed Cleary felt the two women established some sort of connection and Cleary didn't want to risk insinuating anything, in case they would have to question Amari later.

"Samael Skinner. You know they call it Skinner's Woods because of what he tried to do to me out there."

Their silent conversation continued. Then Loust inquired, "I was under the impression he died by drowning?"

Anger pulsed in Amari. If she had one more person tell her that, she thought she might snap. "His body was never found. Now, as soon as I get back into town, I have people trying to break into my house, and then a young girl is killed in the exact place in the exact way he tried to kill me. Open your eyes, rook."

Cleary jumped to Loust's defense. "Ma'am, we don't think the two are related. The Sheriff just wanted us to let you know so you would not be caught off guard hearing it somewhere else."

Amari realized she was fighting a losing battle. These deputies were just following orders. She also understood that neither had been around for her attack. They didn't know the whole story. To them, the fact his body was never found meant very little. To them, it was just another campfire ghost story, a cautionary tale meant to warn young kids about the dangers of going into the woods at night. Maybe some even suggested, as they did when it happened, that it was a lesson about the perils of premarital sex. Which had never been the case.

"Thank you for telling me," Amari said. "I need to get back to work around here."

The two deputies nodded before walking out. Amari would have escorted them, but it was not until they were out of the house that she realized her body was still glued to the counter. Her hands ached from the tightness of her grip.

No one might believe her. Yet, she knew. He was back. He was going to try to finish what he had started. She would not be as unprepared as she had been before. Her body was released from the counter with the jarring realization she needed to take action. It was obvious to Amari that she was on her own in this situation. She removed the bracelet on her left arm and set it on the table. Her plan wasn't formed yet, but she had a vague idea of how to create an early alarm system. The bracelet, which her mother had given her for her confirmation, would only hinder her efforts. Besides, Amari did not want to risk damaging it.

# 17

Amari knew she had several hours to kill before Andrew would be done with work for the day, and come out to help her pack up the house. She dressed quickly, grabbed her holstered gun and a pocket knife, and slid them into the band of her jean shorts before heading out the back door. As she closed it, her eyes were instantly drawn to the distant tree line. The feeling of being watched was now gone, but the comfort it brought was fleeting. There was still an uneasiness she couldn't quite place.

The woods on the property took up only a couple of acres. In the late fall and winter, when the branches were bare, she could see through the entire forest patch to the next plot of land. Despite the passing years, she didn't think the density of the woods would have changed significantly. It wouldn't be an unmanageable area to search.

She thought she remembered most of the areas that opened more than others, as well as the location of thicker growths. She even believed she remembered where the thorned plants used to be. However, she realized changes on the floor of the forested plot would be more drastic than the trees. She decided to walk through the woods to confirm what had changed. The possibility that this information might save her life was worth considering.

Amari crossed the yard to the tree line, finding an opening wide enough for her to go in without getting herself tangled in the underbrush.

Once she vanished into the woods, a wave of unease washed over her. Anxiety surged through different parts of her body—tightness in her stomach and neck, a racing heart, followed by a sharp pain in her neck that radiated outward, making it hard to swallow. She let her eyes close as she started taking deep breaths. Some of the apprehension faded, but a weighted piece of iron still lay chained in her stomach.

After a few more moments, her mind calmed down enough for her to notice that, beyond the initial line of trees, the woods opened. Someone could be two feet from the edge of the woods with an entire camp set up, and anyone outside would have a difficult time seeing it. Especially at night. Ideas began running through her mind—a trap of some sort would probably be her best bet. Alternatively, an alarm system could work. Something she could set up quickly with minimal hassle yet be enough it would alert her to someone lurking on this side of the trees.

She even considered setting snares in the areas a person would most likely pass through. While they wouldn't harm the intruder, she hoped that the confusion and urgency to free themselves would create enough noise to alert her of their presence in case the initial system failed.

As she continued walking the length of the trees, she suddenly stopped. Something caught her attention near one of the wider trees. She knelt as she began brushing debris away with her hand carefully, disturbing only what she wanted to be moved.

There was a slight indentation in the dirt, as though a knee had been placed there to stabilize someone. About three feet higher on the trunk of the tree, something had pulled free a patch of vines, creating a space for a hand to help stabilize. Whoever it had been tried to cover the dirt with old leaves and had even attempted to place the torn vine back in place to make it less obvious. Most others had fallen free or withered, but this one had been deliberately positioned to minimize the visibility of the break.

Amari stood up, an eerie silence enveloping the woods. She felt incredibly alone. Was he there now? Was he watching her?

Breaking out of the woods, she kept her eyes fixed on the trees in front of her, her mind racing with ideas for her alarm system. As she approached the house, she thought something looked off. Amari wished she could place it, but since she couldn't, she shifted her focus back to planning.

Just as she reached the backdoor, she knew what had seemed off to her. The back door was open. Just a crack, but she distinctly remembered listening for the latch to click. She pulled her gun from its home at her hip. Gripping the knob, she struggled from the sweat on her palm. Finally, she was able to open the latch. With her foot, she opened the door fully.

She found herself yet again clearing the house methodically. Nothing appeared to have been touched, or at least, nothing was noticeably disturbed. For a moment, she thought about reporting it, but she suspected nothing would come of it. It would only serve as more evidence to the Sheriff's Department that she was a deranged lunatic.

Amari walked to the kitchen and placed her gun on the table. She used her hands to rub the stress from her face, but she could feel her muscles tightening as she did. Sitting down, she rested her left hand on the grip of her gun, while her right hand reached for the bracelet her mother had given her. However, all her fingers found was the bare table.

# 18

Amari sat on the couch, desperate to allow her body a chance to relax, which only allowed her mind to hover on all the what-ifs blending with endless malignant possibilities her mind could create when left on its own. She decided to try to put her busy mind to work by making lists. Unfortunately, each one centered on where Samael could have been hiding for the past two decades, why he waited so long to start killing, and especially how did he know she was back in town? She tossed the pen, contemplating packing the last of the knick-knacks instead. The moment she ran out of excuses not to, she went to the garage. She began her search on the racks to the far wall.

It took her a few minutes before she found her father's binoculars. After changing into jeans, she strapped her gun and the binoculars to opposite hips. Amari went to her car, locking the front door first. Then she checked it three times. At last, she went to her car and gave a turn to the key allowing the engine to fire to life.

Most of the drive felt like she was on autopilot. When she arrived at the turnoff a mile away, she passed a cluster of white vans, police vehicles, and blacked-out SUVs. She recognized the SUVs as federal. Probably FBI or U.S. Marshals. She had the realization she did not remember most of the drive there. She slowed to go around the cluster of vehicles, watching the federal agents file into their SUVs in an oddly synchronized form. She wondered if they practiced their exits. They drove off in the direction Amari had just come from.

The deputies had told Amari they thought the murder was an isolated incident, in no way tied to the sick bastard killing women along the I-65 corridor. Apparently, she thought, now the feds believed the same thing. Something about the murder was different enough that even federal boys didn't want to touch it. They were always licking their chops to be on the front lines of high-profile cases, the first to take over an investigation, and the first to call the press conferences.

Amari followed the road another two miles before coming to a spot to pull off. The trees hugged tight to the road. She smiled when she was able to find a spot where the trees backed up just enough to allow her to park. She was not entirely sure she would not be hit by a passing car, but her options were severely limited.

Amari ventured into the expansive forest ten feet, then stood still. She knew the crime scene was to her right, and the river would be in the same direction. She knew a mile between where she stood and the scene the trail branched off. Following the river to the scene would take her a full day if she headed north now. Instead, she decided she would head northeast until she hit the point—the local make-out spot for all the teens or a star-gazing paradise for the rising astronomers. From there, she would be able to look down at the scene with minimal risk of being spotted by the detectives. However, she wasn't sure how wide their search grid would be. That, she decided, was a problem she would deal with once she got there.

A hundred yards from the point, she slowed her pace. As she took a step, she stood still for a millisecond to ensure she wasn't alerting anyone to her position. She also had to be sure she would not fall in either open dirt or on moist leaves. She couldn't hear any chatter from where she stood. Better yet, no dogs barking to alert their trainers of her presence. She started climbing the point from the west, using the narrow tree trunks to help pull herself up. The hill was not overly steep, but it was high. She knew if she stepped on a rock, it could be slippery enough to send her tumbling into the dirt below, which from this height could easily break a leg. Then she would be out here alone with no one to help. Amari kept low at the top of the point, thankful she had not fallen and equally grateful she had not been caught.

From her position, Amari began to look around for things she recognized. The point had once been a barren rock with an unobstructed view of the skies. Now, however, tree tops covered the heavens from anyone who may have wanted to watch the dazzling sparkles or fleeting comets dashing across the black canvas of the night sky. She remembered kids used to cut down any growing trees surrounding the point so they could keep the sights and romance at a premium. It was clear to her now not many people went there anymore. At least not for any other reason than to tell her story and prove their bravery by going into the woods alone. Boys would tell the story to get the girls to cling to them and harass the weakest in the group.

Amari scanned to the east until she spotted movement. She pulled the binoculars from their pouch at her hip. She rotated the dial in the middle before addressing the two at the eyepieces. She felt herself becoming frustrated at how long the process was taking. Then, without warning, she was looking at a magnified view of the investigation below.

She spotted the victim tucked under a white sheet with a group of three men and a woman preparing to load the body onto a stretcher board to be carried out. Other members of the forensic team were digging through the dirt, jotting down notes. A man, along with another woman, whom she figured to be detectives, were pointing in different directions, talking. Probably recreating the events of the previous night out loud. Re-telling the story the evidence had told them.

"Poor girl," Amari sighed to herself.

Amari moved her attention back to the white sheet. Though nature had reclaimed most of the old fallen log, she could never forget that place. The girl had been killed in nearly the same spot Samael had found her hiding when she was seventeen. The same spot where he had put his knife to her throat.

Amari's shoulder began to throb with an intensifying heat. She clenched it tightly, applying as much pressure as she could. She broke her focus from the magnified vision rolling onto her back. She tucked her lip between her teeth to bite the pain away. The pain began radiating from the scar into her neck as her heart rate picked up. She tried to swallow but couldn't. Her first instinct was to scream out to the police below, hoping she could do so loud enough for them to find her. Her father's face popped up into her mind. Instinctively, she knew she was having a heart attack.

Unexpectedly, she heard her own voice correct the thought. "Panic attack."

Amari closed her eyes tightly as she began taking deep breaths. As she slowed her breathing to a controllable pace, she began thinking of four things she could touch, three things she could see, two she could smell, then ending with one she could hear. The pain in her neck slowly began to fade silencing the drumming in her chest. She opened her eyes, laying there a moment longer. She looked up through the leaves at the deep blue of the sky, which reminded her of a crystal-clear pool on a hot summer day. Revitalizing.

"I want to go home," she told the emptiness.

*You are the bravest girl I know* she heard her father say from somewhere deep in her mind. The words were so clear it startled her. She sat up, looking around because she was certain someone had to be with her on the point. The same instinct warning her of the impending heart attack told her she was alone despite the crispness of the disembodied voice she heard with her ears, not her mind. Or she thought she had heard.

Amari grabbed the binoculars from the rock, focusing her attention north to the river, only forty yards ahead of her. She scanned the banks, stopping where the police thought Samael Skinner had gone into the river. The river wasn't as full as it had been that night. Even so, it was one of the narrowest points in the stretch of river around the area. It was also one of the calmest.

She let the binoculars drift left. She saw a man, probably in his mid-thirties, fishing with a young boy of around eight. She could see the boy laughing before breaking into a silly dance. The jig sent the father into a laughing fit. She watched, wondering what they would do if they knew what had happened just seventy-five yards from them.

The man and boy slowly morphed into an image of her and her father. He used to take her fishing along the river every couple of weeks. Some of her happiest memories—splintered in with her worst—all happened along the very same bank. It was interesting, she thought, that one place can be entwined with so many drastically different emotional triggers.

She heard her father's voice again.

*"Do you know what it means to be brave, Mari?"*

*"When you aren't scared of anything!"*

*He smiled at her as he put his hand on her shoulder. "No, Mari, that is not what being brave is. Being brave is when you are scared, so scared you just want to run away, but you face the thing that scares you anyway."*

*Amari thought about what he had said for a moment. She was scared when she saw a snake once. She ran; she hadn't faced the snake. "I guess I'm not very brave."*

*"Why would you say that?"*

*"Remember the snake I saw once? It scared me so much I ran away."*

*Her father nodded his head and smiled. "It doesn't mean you're not brave. It just means at the moment, running away was the better option. At that moment, it was. Do you remember the other day at the playground?"*

*Amari thought intently. Despite the focused thought, she could not recall the time he referred to. Every time she had been at the playground blended in her mind. She couldn't remember a time she had ever been scared there. She shook her head.*

*"You wanted to do the monkey bars but they were just a little too high for you. You asked me ten times to help you because you thought you might get hurt. I just sat there telling you to go for it. You jumped and grabbed the bars, then went straight across. That was being brave. Then, when your friends and you were afraid to slide down the pole, you were the first one to try. That was being brave. You feared what might happen because of how high it was. You went for it anyway. You are the bravest girl I know."*

*Amari beamed with pride as she leaned into her dad.*

Amari pulled the binoculars from her eyes, rubbing at the tears. She cleared the stone forming in the center of her throat before returning her eyes to the eyepiece.

She turned her focus beyond the nearby bank to the other side of the river. As she continued her scan, she spotted a void in the hill. Her head shot back, but she struggled to find it again. She slowly scanned the bank until she saw it.

The void was a cave. It looked like it could have gone deep into the hill. Even with the binoculars at full magnification, it was impossible to tell. The shadows from the trees cast just enough darkness in front of the entrance, creating an empty abyss.

Many caves in the area went deep into the earth, some close to a hundred feet. She didn't think that one would be as expansive as some, but she felt the need to check. Amari knew the odds of her finding anything would be slim. From her experience, she knew the police had not checked the other side of the river after her attack. They were so certain Samael could not have made it across they thought the idea was an "unjust and foolish waste of manpower and resources." If they thought that girl had been killed in the spot where her body fell, or even if they thought the killer had brought her into the woods from the same side, they would see no need to search the cave either.

A startling thought crossed her mind. What if he had been watching the girl from the cave? What if he had gone in there to watch the investigation? What if he were watching them now?

Amari scanned the river for a shallow spot to cross. A resolve sparked deep in her gut.

# 19

Amari spotted a shallow area in the river twenty yards to the west of the fishermen. The river was also narrower here, with three large rocks protruding from the water's surface that would allow her to cross with mostly dry feet. She gave a glance to the fishermen, but they were lost in their nirvana, barely noticing her presence. With the river behind her, she headed east toward the mouth of the cave. Amari glanced over at the fishermen again, satisfied they were preoccupied with tying on new lures, and again they paid her no attention.

At the face of the void Amari brought up her flashlight from her front pocket. She flicked the button on the back twice to get to the brightest setting before twisting the light end to expand the focal point of the rays. It was now or never. The truth, one way or another, would be inside.

Upon entering Amari stopped in amazement at how deceptive the mouth of the cave had been. The opening was only five feet high and about three feet wide. However, once inside, the cave opened to double or triple the size. Amari could see the cave went twenty yards into the hill before dropping off and then branching off to the right. Even with the brightness of the light coupling with the larger focal point, the cave was overwhelmingly dark. Even in its openness, she felt claustrophobic, as if the walls were slowly closing in on her, ready to consume her.

As she pressed forward, Amari noticed trash littered the corners she could see. She wondered if it had been used as a hangout or camping spot. Or if animals had brought the litter in to make nests. She continued back to the ledge of the drop-off, relieved to see the ledge was only three feet above the next level. The passage branching to the right appeared to narrow further ahead, but she couldn't see beyond about ten feet. She decided to concentrate on the immediate area.

Scanning the beam of her flashlight along the ledge, she stopped at the cave wall to her right. Water seemed to be seeping in, casting a glittery reflection on the rock walls. Something in the bottom corner of her vision stole her attention. It was a dark maroon cloth, clearly not a natural part of the cave.

Amari compelled her legs to take her up to the deep red item. She kneeled just inches from it—It was a pile of discarded clothing. Appearing as though the clothing had been tucked away there for quite some time. Amari extended her flashlight to prod the pile with the front of the light to make sure nothing would come rushing out to defend its home. After a few pokes, she felt confident no bloodthirsty beasts would be flying out with snarled teeth and exposed claws ready to do battle.

Placing her flashlight into the thickest part of the cloth, she pulled it free from its place along the wall. She put the flashlight in her mouth, holding it between her lips to keep it in place, and pulled the cloth up, letting it fall open, dirt and decaying leaves falling to the cave floor.

As the garment opened, the cave's coolness turned even colder, sending a shiver through her. She recognized the sweatshirt, it's deep red etched into her memory like a treasured photograph. It was the same shirt—she was certain of it—he had worn when he attacked her. Brown stains around the back of the collar resembled old blood spots. She had hit him in the head with a rock; she knew without a doubt that head wounds bled profusely.

"This was his," she confirmed for herself.

Familiar doom settled deep in her stomach, pushing her toward nausea. The cave floor seemed to tilt in different directions, making her feel off-balance. The sensation faded almost as quickly as it had arisen. For a moment, she considered taking the sweatshirt to the police for testing.

"No," she condemned herself for the thought.

She knew the game. Even if they indulged her by taking it, it could be weeks or months—if ever—before they ran it through the system. If they did test it, the year-round stability of the temperature of the cave would have preserved the DNA, but animals and moisture would have the opposite effect. They would most likely discard the garment, convinced Amari was out of her mind and that Samael could have never made it to the cave. Or it would be too contaminated by squatters or animals to waste their time.

"Maybe they will test it. Then I will know for sure."

"Except you know they won't," Amari countered with herself.

"I don't know that," her eyes became glued to the fabric, unable to break free.

"Yes, you do. You don't need a test to prove what you already know."

What she already knew was someone was out there watching her.

Someone was waiting for her.

She could taste it. In the deepest parts of her soul, she could feel it.

# 20

Upon returning home, Amari felt as though every bit of life she possessed had faded away. Exhaustion weighed her down, and even the energy required to keep her eyes open had become overwhelming. During the drive home, she fantasized about her bed while the voices in the recesses of her mind refused to remain quiet about the sweatshirt tucked away in the cave. Even if he had died, it wasn't the way the police had said. He hadn't been washed away in the river. At least not that night.

Amari parked her car, being met with a mix of revitalized and apprehension at the sight of Andrew's truck. She wanted to leap from her car and confide in him about everything she had found. Somehow, she resisted the urge. Amari didn't think she could bare his skeptical gaze or his voice of reason now. Not right now. The doubt in his eyes, that cutting glare, would undermine her. How long could he keep doubting her? Eventually, like anyone else, he would grow weary of her paranoia.

Anyone else would.

Amari got out of the car, making sure she left the sweatshirt. The nagging voice saying, *He will think you've lost all sense of reality*, had won. She realized that if she were to show him the shirt or confess her venture to the crime scene, he would dismiss her entirely.

"Hey," he sang as he stood from the steps of the front porch. He was walking toward her. "I was getting worried. Where did you go?"

"A couple of deputies came by this morning. They told me a girl was murdered last night. Told me they 'didn't want me to be alarmed' because it happened right where I was attacked."

His reaction was unexpected, devoid of surprise or shock. Instead, his expression conveyed sympathy—a look Amari had come to despise because it meant others pitied her.

"You already knew that, didn't you?" Amari crossed her chest with her arms. "Because everyone in this town knows every little thing about everything."

Andrew placed his hands on her arms from a slight distance, holding her gently but not too closely. The contact felt awkward, as if an invisible barrier formed between them and he had come as close as he could. "It's why I was worried. I tried calling you all day. You never answered."

"I was out in the woods. I probably didn't have any service." Regret instantly followed her words; she hadn't meant to speak them. Andrew stepped back.

"What woods?"

"*The* woods. Skinner's Woods."

Andrew's eyes expanded with disbelief. "Why in the world would you do that?"

"I had to see it for myself," she spoke matter-of-factly, though even to her, the words sounded hollow. They lacked the truth about what she had hoped to gain from seeing the site. Of course, she recognized; she was not sure what she hoped to find there in the first place.

"Why? Why would you want to?"

Amari shook her head. She hadn't expected him to understand, but she had hoped he would feign understanding, if only for her. Her face felt warm. Her teeth clenched so tightly that her jaw began to ache. Storming off to her car, she was determined to prove herself right. She could feel his presence. It was almost tangible. Unlocking her car, she reached inside for the sweatshirt, debating with herself. She still had a chance to turn back, to avoid revealing the shirt. She might save herself from ridicule if she stopped now. However, as gracefully as a dancer, she spun around, casting the sweater into his hands. It was done; there was no turning back. Andrew unfolded the cloth to better examine it with noticeable displeasure. "What am I looking at?"

"His sweatshirt." The look on Andrew's face told Amari she would have to spell it out for him. In Andrew's mind, Samael was dead, and with him, everything that happened to her. "Samael's sweatshirt. It is the same one he was wearing the night he attacked me."

Andrew bit his lip, first from the left, then from the right. He went back and forth examining the shirt for what seemed like hours. "Amari, a lot of people around here have this exact same shirt. It is one of the biggest universities in the state, not to mention the closest. Everyone in town has their merchandise."

"What about the blood stains? On the front where he was pressed against me. Also, on the back, where his head wound would have bled onto. How do you explain those?"

He handed the shirt back to her. "Where did you find it?"

"In a cave opposite the river from where he attacked me. Where the police said he was swept in?"

Andrew nodded, his expression signaling that he had an explanation. But more than that, it held concern. Amari was right; he thought she hadn't just gone off the deep end but had performed a swan dive straight onto the rocks below. "Maybe it came off in the river. Some animals carried it in to use as a nest. Or it was some hunter who left it in there. That blood—if that's even what it is— could have come from anywhere."

Amari felt more alone than she had in a long time. The emptiness in her stomach radiated through her body with the sting of a thousand bees. "Why are you so fucking confident he died in the river?"

His expression turned pained, and a part of Amari was glad for it. Yet, another, deeper part of her felt ashamed.

"Because I was out in those woods with the search parties for a week. Dogs, choppers, and hundreds of volunteers. No one ever found so much as a shoe print at the place on the bank he was supposed to have gone in at. I personally checked several caves. They were all empty. If I had found him, I would have killed him myself. So, yes, Amari. I am sure he did not come out of the river."

Amari lowered her head. "I didn't know you did all of that. I'm sorry. I just thought…"

Andrew took a step toward her. "Believe me, he is dead. Whoever attacked the girl was not Samael Skinner. Maybe it was the same sick bastard they'd been looking for. Maybe it was a coincidence. Either way, it was *not* him." Amari didn't understand how he could be so certain of his belief.

With a heavy sigh, Amari released pent-up tension, feeling a flood of apprehension surge. "I don't know what the hell is going on, Andrew. I feel like I'm losing my damn mind."

"Look, you spent your whole life trying to get away from this place and all the terrible things you had happen to you here. This place is Hell on Earth to you. Anyone that's been through as much shit as you would feel the exact same way." He pulled her close, enveloping her in his embrace. Then he stepped back and walked toward the house, pausing midway between his previous position and the porch. "Come on, the sooner we pack this place up the sooner you can put it in your rearview."

Amari looked at Andrew, feeling a new yearning within her.

# 21

*Amari followed him through the woods. He had parked in between two trees, serving two purposes: concealing the car from other drivers and protecting it if a drunken fool took the turn too quickly. Amari teased him, suggesting the car might be decimated by a semi while they were hiking through the woods. He laughed and retorted, saying no one drove that road at night. But if they did and crashed into anything, it would be the tree to take the hit and not his car.*

*The walk to the point was too fast. Their conversation during the trek revolved around their plans after graduation. He shared his desire to work at a factory, seeking a steady job with minimal mental demands. A position that would lead to a fat pension, allowing him to eventually explore the world and swim in every ocean. Amari recognized that he was only half serious. He often spoke of traveling the world and living freely, as he believed God intended.*

*Amari was captivated by the idea of adventure, of experiencing the world through different cultures. However, she felt her own path was predetermined. After graduation, she would attend college, embark on a career, get married, and raise children. She aimed to be a better parent than her mom or dad had been. At least, that had been her father's aspiration for her. Amari wanted to stay in New Hope to assist her father with farming and raising her children near him so he could pass down his wisdom.*

*When they reached the point, he took her hand in his. The sky was clear. Every star shimmered majestically. The full moon hung low, casting a brilliant white hue across everything her eyes could see. It didn't look real to her. It looked like one of the paintings in the art gallery in town.*

*At the top of the point, he took her into his arms. He began dancing with her to music only he could hear. "This is going to be a night we'll never forget," he told her.*

*Ever since he had asked her out two weeks before, Amari had been gleaming. He was the boy every girl coveted—popular, funny, and strikingly handsome. Somehow, he had chosen her. Through all her faults and ugliness, he wanted her. He adored her. He had reassured her of his feelings multiple times over the past weeks.*

*The other kids stopped tormenting her. She was no longer the "basehead's daughter." It was ironic because Amari knew for a fact her mom's dealer was the same dealer half of their parents used. Their substances of choice might differ—pills or marijuana instead of heroin—but their secrets were equally dark.*

*Amari watched the moonlight dance across his face. He was the only person, apart from her father, who made her feel safe. The only one who understood her at the deepest level, not just the facade she presented to the world. He saw beyond the mask, the image she projected to convince others of her identity. He knew her more intimately than she knew herself at times.*

*Being in his arms felt like time had paused. At that moment, it was only the two of them. She hoped it would always be that way. Then the reality struck her: in a few months, she would head to college while he would explore the world, encountering exotic women far more beautiful than she was. Women without her tormented history.*

*He would socialize with the rich and famous. Suddenly, whatever allure she held for him would vanish. "What if I went with you?"*

*"Where?" he inquired.*

*"Wherever you are going after college."*

*"You'll be with me forever. In my heart, in my mind, in my memories, and in my dreams. Not a day will pass when I will not think of this perfect night."*

*Amari melted into his embrace, longing for a kiss.*

*Unsurprisingly, he had read her mind. He could always read her mind. He knew her desires before she had even spoken them.*

*Placing his forefinger beneath her chin, he gently lifted her face toward his. Gazing deep into her eyes, he mirrored the calm of the ocean surface. She closed her eyes, anticipating the tenderness of his lips.*

*When his lips touched hers, it was as magical as she had hoped. She felt her heart skip a beat, her stomach fluttering with a wave of emotion—happiness, excitement, pure perfection. Even in her dreams, the kiss had not been this perfect.*

*Then, something suddenly felt wrong. He pulled away abruptly as if her kiss repulsed him. She was afraid to open her eyes and confront the revulsion she anticipated finding on his face. She suddenly felt a sharp pain in her arm, like a flame had ignited beneath her skin. Agony seared through her as if her entire right side were being consumed by the flames. Was this what a heart attack felt like? No, she was too young for a heart attack!*

*A scream tore from her throat as the pain intensified. Her eyes flew open. He was withdrawing a knife from her shoulder. Time seemed to crawl; each fraction elongated as if she were living in a slow-motion scene from a movie. His face, once full of love and tenderness, was now twisted into a grotesque mask of hunger and horror, a monstrous reflection of vile lust. His serene eyes burned with desire—not for her, not the same way they used to.*

*Her father's voice exploded in her head. Out of pure instinct—along with the guidance of the voice in her mind—she swung her leg as hard as she could. She kicked him in the groin. The animalistic scream broke her frozen foot from the rocks allowing her to flee.*

*As she sprinted through the woods, his voice echoed, "It's time to play!"*

Amari jolted awake, a cold sweat coated her body, yet her flesh burned. She scanned the room like she always did after a nightmare. Once assured she was alone, she stood from the bed, undressing from her damp clothing.

She didn't bother checking the time as she headed for the shower. It didn't matter. She knew sleep would elude her for the rest of the night. After her shower, she would retrieve her gun and nestle herself in front of the television until the sun rose.

# 22

At 4 a.m., Amari felt her eyes growing heavy. She had spent the past several hours partially watching old reruns on a channel offering only classic shows. She kept the volume low so she could hear any sounds that might come from outside. Something about the intensity of the nightmare had been worse than the ones before it. She had always stayed up once she awoke from one of the bad dreams. To her, this one felt real, not at all like a dream. As if she were reliving the entire event again.

Her mouth and throat felt sore from their dryness. She got up from the couch to walk to the kitchen sink—she had not wanted to stay upstairs with no exits available. As she stood at the sink filling her cup, something outside caught her attention. It was hard to tell because the lack of moonlight kept the outside near pitch black. She thought she saw something move.

"Relax, it's probably an animal. You didn't hear anyone walking around."

*Maybe the TV was too loud.*

She turned off the water tilting her head slightly so her left ear was facing the window but still allowed her to see outside. Almost at the same time, the motion lights burst to life, illuminating the area, and causing her to jump. At first, the beam revealed to her nothing more than an empty yard. Probably another animal, she thought.

Then just outside of the beam at the edge of the halo of light bleeding out toward the tree line, she saw the shadow running. She could not accurately tell the size of the figure. She could only tell it was a human. They ran parallel with the trees, and then just as they escaped the outer aura of light, they turned into the woods.

"Who the hell..."

Amari dropped her glass in the sink, pulling her gun from her waist. She opened the drawer near her, digging until she found a small flashlight, which would have happened sooner had she investigated the drawer rather than keeping her eyes glued to the entry point in the woods. She wished she had brought her light down with her, but she did not have time to get it now. The figure could have been thirty yards into the woods by then and was moving further away.

She sprinted from the house triggering the floodlights again. It made her vulnerable. An easy target for the figure to scope her if he were armed. She had no cover nor any concealment. All she could do was run to the edge of the woods as fast as she could, hoping he would not take her out before then.

Once in the woods, the floodlights went out, leaving her in total darkness. She didn't want to use her light yet. She wanted to listen. She held hope he would give away his position. Using her light now gave him yet another advantage. Amari felt he had enough.

She held her breath, listening to the natural sounds of the woodlands. Leaves rustled in the soft breeze. Crickets sang melodic songs of romance. An owl called out to its visitors. Then something big moved quickly from her right to left. It did not quite sound big enough to be a person. A raccoon, perhaps?

She raised the barrel of her gun in the direction of the sound. With her left hand, she flipped the flashlight on, maneuvering it to rest between the grip of the gun and her left thumb so she could have sight as well as a steady grip.

The dull yellow hue only went ten feet in front of her. The nearly lifeless beam worked more against her than for her. Where she thought the sound had come from, she saw nothing. Not even the malevolent glow from watchful eyes. She cut the beam off, then slid the flashlight into her pocket. She continued walking deeper into the woods. Her ears perked at every sound.

After ten more feet, she stopped again, holding her breath. Still, she heard nothing but the sounds of the woods. Except now, she felt those watchful eyes on her. They cast a chill through her body, causing the hairs on her neck to stand at attention. Her flesh rose into bumps knowing she was not alone in the woods. Her sight was limited, and with the little bit of concealment she had, she felt too exposed.

Whoever was with her knew the woods better than she did. They were moving without noise. She wasn't sure of the exact moment, just that it wasn't long before she could feel eyes surrounding her from every direction. She was being stalked. She had become the prey.

She turned the gun slightly to its left, lowering it just a couple of inches to give her better visibility. Her eyes were beginning to adapt, which allowed her to see the shapes of trees and plants around her. The shadowed figure was still invisible. She thought she could hear him breathing. Then, before she could listen for where it was coming from, it was gone.

The quietness of the woods was broken by a dark guttural voice. It breathed, "Not time to play yet."

Her body locked up as if it had been restrained by a weight, chained to her legs, pulling her down. It prevented all movement. It even made breathing more difficult. Her mind tried to break her body free from the invisible bondage with no success.

She knew he was behind her. She did not know how he got there without detection, just that he had. Before her mind could process what to do next, she felt a sudden shock at the back of her head. Her ears echoed the deafening thud sound that came with the abrupt pain.

Then the world was dark. Quiet.

# 23

The warmth of the sun against her skin stirred Amari. Though it was the rhythmic knocking of a woodpecker in the distance which forced her eyes open. She was outside. On her back porch. Every part of her body ached, but none as much as her head. She ran her hand over the back of her skull, where she felt the dried blood caked to her hair, which had mixed with dirt and dead leaves. Amari groaned as she fought gravity to raise her body. Pain radiated to new parts of her as she moved. She saw her gun resting in front of her. Amari grabbed it, and released the magazine by muscle memory. Then, once she was assured it was still loaded, she popped the magazine back in. She set it down to her side.

The night before was hazy. She remembered chasing something into the woods, then the abrupt pain in her head. She could have sworn he spoke to her. Had she imagined the whole thing?

The voice was unrecognizable—at least, she couldn't place it. Had she really been attacked? How did she get to the porch? Did he carry her? Had he *touched* her? She forced her mind to be silent as she examined her body. All her clothes were intact, which she thought was a good thing. The pain felt like it had been from sleeping on concrete as much as being hit in the head.

The pain began to fuel a rage inside of her. She had been powerless the night before. She hated the familiar feeling. As if she were a pawn in his little game. Like he controlled her every move. *Game. He had said something about a game.*

Amari rolled to her knees, gently pushing herself up from the ground. She would not be caught off guard again.

Twenty minutes later, she had showered and cleaned her wounds. She dressed in a pair of jeans and an old sweatshirt before putting on her tennis shoes. After her third glass of water, she checked the clock on the stove. 7 a.m. Amari headed out to the garage, where her plan would come together.

She wasted ten minutes rummaging through miscellaneous boxes along with other items her father kept locked away. Guests did not have access to the garage because her father liked to use it for his storage. Most of his hunting equipment and fishing tackle were kept there for his trips to the cabin.

Her father preferred to fish for bass or bluegill. Every so often, in the fall, he would get the itch for catfishing. He had always said it was the best way to test a person's patience. He had believed it was also the best way to fish and allow time to just be. No rushing, not constantly changing lures, not walking from one spot on the bank to the next. Just casting once before letting nature consume him.

Amari dug through the bag until she reached a box at the bottom. She removed it, popping the three tabs around the exterior of the case. She removed seven pole bells her father used to clamp to the end of his rods to alert him to bites.

Then she returned to the bag until she found the spool of fishing line. She gathered everything into her arms. She left the garage through the side door, which allowed access to the area between the detached garage and the house. At the face of the woods, she surveyed the tree line. She could see where he was entering and exiting from, but she could not be certain it had been his only point of entry.

She assumed he had entered the woods from the backside because she would have no view of the field from her house. Then he would navigate the short distance to the spot where overgrowth was the least. The woods were less dense here. If he chose another route since she had spotted him the night before, her plan would be useless.

Amari guessed he would be like any other creature that roamed the woods. They always pick the path of least resistance. The easiest trail is the one they will always travel. Humans were also creatures of habit, she knew; they operate mostly the same every time. He had gotten the best of her the night before. The small victory would make him cocky and overconfident. He would have no reason to think he could not use the same exit point each time.

She lowered herself to her knees and then began unraveling twelve feet of fishing line. She bit the line free from the spool, then tied the bells to it every few feet, careful not to tangle the line together. Once she was sure the bells were secure, she gave a flick to the line. They were not startlingly loud. Part of Amari wondered if she would even hear them from the house. It was better than nothing, she rationalized to the more critical thoughts. If nothing else, it might startle whoever had been in the woods, and he would make enough noise to betray his location all on his own.

Amari tied one end of the line to the base of a young tree, then pulled the line taught, latching it to another tree nine feet away. She made sure the bells were all low enough they would not stand out yet still high enough to swing freely without being obstructed by the grass or fallen twigs.

Once she was sure her alarm system worked, she began covering the line with leaves and other debris lying around the area. The backside of the bells were all hidden in case he used a light.

Amari had hoped having the trap set would make her feel more secure. To her dissatisfaction, it did not. She knew if he wanted to get to her, he could. He would. This might buy her some time, although she doubted it would deter him.

"Amari!" Andrew's voice was distant, up near the cabin.

Amari looked down at the alarm system once more. Mostly satisfied with its concealment, she started walking back toward the house.

"Down here," she shouted. As she walked back toward the house she glanced back at the woods, wondering if he was watching her now.

Amari rounded the house to find Andrew standing by his truck. The confusion on his face when he saw her made Amari stop. She looked down at herself. She thought for a moment she had forgotten to put on shoes or, worse, had put on mismatched shoes. She had some dirt on her jeans. Otherwise, nothing stood out. The tension between them yesterday had ended with Andrew apologizing for dismissing her fear. Which then led to her apologizing for acting irrationally. In the end, she knew he still did not believe her, and she only further questioned herself.

"Why are you covered in dirt?" he asked.

"I would hardly call this *covered*," she retorted. There had been times in her childhood when it had been hard to tell if she was clothed at all or just coated in thick layers of mud.

"More than most people cleaning out a house."

"Oh, I saw a deer." She remembered how alone she felt when she had shown him the sweatshirt the day before. Amari knew if she told him she had been setting alarms or even about the attack the night before, he would placate her just to avoid making her upset. "I followed it into the woods to get a better look."

"You grew into a full-blown city girl, huh," he teased with a smile.

She continued up to his truck, taking a spot beside him as he pulled two bundles of boxes toward himself. They were secured with thin white plastic straps. He retrieved a knife from his pocket to cut them free of the confines. She noticed the knife was brand new. The color of the plastic handle was vibrant and fresh.

"Didn't you used to have an old knife you carried on your belt?" She wasn't sure how she remembered the detail. Nothing about it stuck out. She knew her father often had a handful of knives he would rotate through.

"Yeah," he said, looking down at the new blade in his hand. He seemed frustrated. "I think I lost the damn thing. Couldn't find it anywhere. I'll have to check the construction site tomorrow."

He cut the boxes from their binds so he could begin unstacking them. He handed her one, "Shall we pack up the linens you won't be needing? The church said they would love to have them."

"You lead the way."

# 24

The heat of the day thickened relentlessly, suffocating them as they worked. The air in the cabin began to feel like a sauna, forcing Amari to stop every third trip from the house to the truck to ensure she wouldn't become too dehydrated. No matter how hard she tried, she couldn't escape the relentless intensity of the rising temperature. She found herself watching Andrew in astonishment as he kept moving. He seemed completely unfazed by the scorch.

"How can this heat not bother you?"

"I've worked in construction my whole life. This is a cool day."

"A cool day? It must be a record high!"

Andrew laughed as he tossed another box into the bed of his truck. "Try insulating an attic on a day like today. Then you'll sing a different song." Andrew walked up to her. She handed him her bottle of water. He took a hard swig, but as soon as the water entered his mouth, it seemed to just come out of his skin. She felt drawn to him as an unseen pull from him gripped her. She could not describe nor deny the power in the tug.

She stood up, resting her hand on his arm. Amari slid her hand down to his, gripping the outside of his palm gently. She thought he may have felt the same lure that pulled at her. What worried her was that she was still afraid she had convinced him she was the living embodiment of Winona Ryder in *Girl, Interrupted*, destined for a psych ward where she would be locked away from the normal people outside.

"Thank you for all your help. I don't think I could've done all this alone."

His eyes fell low to meet hers, consuming her gratitude. They told her he was happy to be there with her. They told her he looked forward to their days together and maybe he hoped they would never end. Then Amari pulled her gaze away. She felt a familiar sting of shame. She had no idea if that was what he had been thinking. She felt her mind bouncing from wall to wall, never able to quite find the truth, only what she thought the truth might be in a single moment. Either he thought she was crazy or he cared for her. Amari couldn't decide which of the truths she had created was real

Andrew put a gentle hand on her cheek, summoning her eyes back to face him. The same tenderness still shined in his eyes. "I have been waiting for you to come back for a long time."

The words entered her mind one at a time as a thickness filled her chest. The overwhelming heat that had already stifled her breathing grew heavier, forcing the words to echo in her ears. She thought she might suffocate in it. Before she could process the words fully, she heard tires in the gravel driveway only a few yards from where they stood.

Both she and Andrew turned to the sound. A Sheriff's patrol car had parked, and a woman exited the vehicle. Amari thought she recognized the woman, but the polarized Aviator Sunglasses hid the woman's eyes, as the Campaign Hat hid most of the top portion of her face.

"Sheriff, what brings you out this way?" Andrew asked. Amari thought she heard a glimmer of concern escape his lips.

Amari felt herself pull her hand from Andrew's without intent as if they had just been caught doing something they shouldn't have been. The clamminess in her flesh morphed into an iced chill. First the deputies, now the Sheriff. What else had happened? Did they find who had killed that poor girl?

The woman stopped just feet in front of them, removing her thick sunglasses. Amari saw the woman's unobstructed face, finally recognizing her. Trishia Lexington, though her name badge now read Benning. Amari could never forget her. From the time they were babies until the attack, they were best friends. At one time, they had been inseparable. Where one was found the other was sure to be nearby.

Trishia had been one of only a few people Amari had confided in about her mom's addiction. One of the only people besides her father she could turn to after her death. The only one she could cry in front of. Trishia had been a rock for her. A place of solid ground in a world she felt was consumed by quicksand.

Trishia had a crush on Samael Skinner. All the girls did. It was when he asked Amari out that things changed. Trishia felt betrayed—though she had never told Amari she liked him—and like so many people, she blamed Amari for what had happened to her.

*Well, if she wasn't such a slut... She just brings trouble... She probably killed him and stabbed herself to get away with it...*

"Amari," Trishia flashed a broad smile. Amari knew it was disingenuous.

"Trish, I didn't know you were the Sheriff. Congratulations." Amari's throat felt dry. Her tongue scraped the inside of her mouth like sandpaper as she spoke. She took a drink of water but the graininess didn't wash away. Somehow, it felt worse

"Voted in a couple of years ago. I was just following in my best pal's footsteps."

*Best pal.* Amari held back a laugh. She didn't need to bring any more unwanted issues her way. "I was not expecting to see anyone from your department after the last time. Is everything okay?"

Trishia shrugged, moving her attention to Andrew. "That's what I am here to find out. Your foreman told me I could find you here."

"What could you possibly need to talk to me about?" Andrew's tone was more defensive than Amari expected. She could sense the tension weighing the already suffocating air down more. She wasn't sure if it came from them or between her and Trishia, but it was expanding.

Trishia turned to Amari with a patronizing smirk. Amari had a flashback of wanting to smack the look from her face. Her hands clenched almost instinctively. She had to force them open again. "You really know how to pick 'em, Mari."

"You can call me Amari. And what the hell is that supposed to mean?" The words were bitter. Now she was the defensive one. She did not care to hide it in any way. The deep radiating resentment came storming back as if she were seventeen again. Vengeful, perhaps even still damaged just as much as she ever had been.

Trishia's attention went back to Andrew. "We found a knife near the body. It is your knife," she pulled a plastic bag from her back pocket with a blood-stained blade inside. The date was penned above some coordinates on the outside in marker. She held the bag up in front of Amari and Andrew. "This is yours. Is it not?"

Andrew looked down at Amari. His eyes promised his innocence. They were full of shock, which slowly morphed into fear. They told her everything she needed to know.

Just as Andrew was about to speak, Amari interrupted. "Don't answer that," she barked.

"What, are you his lawyer now?"

"Obviously not. I still won't let you try to railroad him. He told me this morning his knife had been stolen. Anyone who had access to it at any of his construction sites could have taken it. Anyone who had access to his home. Are you questioning them, too?"

Trisha's posture stiffened as she closed the gap between them. "I don't answer to you."

"Lucky you."

Trishia turned toward Andrew as she gingerly returned the knife to her back pocket. "You are going to have to come with me to the station. Turn around."

"Is he under arrest?"

Trishia ignored the question, latching the cuffs. Andrew seemed to be drifting somewhere else, remaining silent until Trishia tightened the cuffs more, causing him to grunt.

"If he is under arrest, you have to Mirandize him."

"I know the law, Amari. No, he is not under arrest. Yet. Now back up."

"I'll follow you to the station," she promised Andrew.

"You need to stay here. We will be questioning him. Since you're not his attorney, you have no right to be there."

Amari jogged up beside Andrew. "Do not say a single word. Ask for your lawyer, and do not speak a syllable until they get there."

"Back off before I arrest you for obstruction!" Trishia barked the words like an angry mutt. Amari stepped aside, watching helplessly as Trishia forced Andrew into the back seat, slamming the door on his freedom as much as she did on him.

"Not a word," Amari said again. Andrew didn't acknowledge her instructions; his eyes lasered the back of Trishia's headrest as he tried to make sense of the situation.

When the patrol car was out of sight, Amari opened the door to Andrew's truck. She grabbed the keys he had left in the ignition, then she locked the door, even though she doubted he had anything worth stealing in the old rusting vehicle. The aged white Ford was like several others in town, though to Andrew, it had some unobvious quality about it he loved.

Amari could feel her anxiety ramping up as she prepared to leave. If she was not there, she would be the most vulnerable. If someone was watching her, playing some sick game with her, they would have unlimited access while she was gone. In her experience, that could be hours.

# 25

Amari went from one window to the next, making sure each one was secured. She also made sure the doors were all locked, even the garage door outside. She grabbed an empty duffle bag from the master bedroom, tossing in a couple of water bottles as well as small snacks. She was not sure how long she might have to wait for the interrogation to end. Depending on what evidence they had connecting Andrew to the murder, she could be there well into the night. If they were zeroed in on Andrew it could even stretch into tomorrow. With the tension between her and Trishia, she doubted anyone at the station would be forthcoming about how long they expected the process to be.

Part of her also knew—as much as she tried to deny it to herself—she was stalling. The thought of leaving, not being there to hear the bells, scared her. If someone was watching her now, they would know she was planning to leave. They would know there would be unrestricted access to her home. As hard as she tried to force the images of a stranger in her home away, the mental slide show of the thought would not leave.

When she could stall no more, she walked to the front door and then turned to ensure the house was empty one final time. She was sure Andrew had nothing to do with the murder. She vaguely remembered the voice in the woods. It had said something about a game, that much she was sure of. If this psychopath wanted to play games, what better way could they get to her than to hurt the people she cared about? The only one they had access to was Andrew. It was all part of his game.

*Unless you imagined it*, the annoying voice which was her own reminded her silently.

"I didn't," she rebuked.

Amari finally forced herself outside. She locked the door, checking its resolve twice before heading down to her car. She opened the trunk to toss her duffle bag inside. Once she closed the lid of the trunk, she knew there was nothing else keeping her. Amari trudged to the driver's side door and slid in, noticing the rearview mirror was tilted in such a way she could only see the ceiling. She thought back to the last time she had driven the car. With near certainty, she didn't think she had bumped it. Amari never hung things from the mirror, which may have caused it to move either.

Frustrated, she grabbed the edge of the rearview mirror arranging it in a way that would allow her to see oncoming vehicles.

As she shifted the plastic of the mirror, she thought she caught sight of something in the bottom left corner. Something dark obscured the gray leather of her backseat. The only thing she ever kept in the backseat was a 24-hour survival bag in case of breakdowns. It was a bright orange bag she kept on the floor behind the passenger seat with no reason to have been moved.

She adjusted the mirror more, pulling it toward her and downward. In the mirror, she saw the reflection of Samael Skinner. His face was pale, a colorless palette. His eyes sunken in, surrounded by deep black rings of weariness, which only added depth to the voids. The eyes projected coldness, malice, anger, and a thirst for her, just as they had twenty years before. His face was expressionless though somehow it screamed at her.

Amari couldn't comprehend the sight at first. She stared at it for a second before the vision registered in her mind. Without control of her voice, she screamed as she slammed her body into the door, causing it to fly open. Her momentum carried her outward, forcing her to crash into the rocky driveway. She slid a few inches before scrambling to her feet, simultaneously drawing her pistol from her waistband holster.

She pointed the gun out as her eyes narrowed on the sights, which focused on the center of the rear window. As she stared down at the light green bead at the front of the gun, she found the window to be the only target. She left the barrel aimed at the window as she quickly scanned beyond the car. The openness of the property meant she would see anyone fleeing on foot. Still, she saw nothing. Amari approached the vehicle vigilantly, lowering her body enough to be able to see straight through the window closest to her and out of the other.

The backseat was empty. The door was still firmly latched. Amari dropped to her stomach, pointing the gun directly under the car. The other side was void of human life as well.

Amari slowly forced herself to her feet. "What the fuck?!" She screamed the words as loudly as she could. Then as she felt the tension within her reaching catastrophic levels, just screamed. It helped, though not as much as she wanted it to.

"What is happening to me? I am losing my fucking mind! I need to just leave. I can leave and hire someone else to do this shit."

The voice in Amari's head spoke back to her. *No. That's what he wants.*

"I can't keep doing this. I'm spiraling."

*You are playing his game.*

"I don't want to play any games! Do you hear me?! I'm not playing your games!"

*Then make him play yours.*

Amari began to gather herself. "Play mine?" She whispered the words to the air.

*You make the rules. Make him play your game.*

Amari holstered her pistol, allowing her to get into the car. "Play my game," she repeated to herself. She checked the rearview mirror again. The car was empty, just as it had been when she first got in. She saw the redness in her eyes growing around the moisture that had risen from the bottom of her eyelid. She wiped her eyes dry, shaking the voice away.

At the end of the driveway, Amari thought about turning right. It would take her away from town and eventually back home. She could leave. Hardly anyone would notice at all. She could leave this town once and for all, along with everything that came with it. She could wash her hands of every memory plus all the foul darkness the town reminded her of.

Then she thought of Andrew. She couldn't leave him alone. Not now. Not when he needed her the most. There was little she would be able to do for him, but she could be a support. She could be the one person in town who didn't believe he was a killer.

Amari knew how New Hope worked. She knew how they could turn on someone like a pack of feral dogs circling before attacking the weakest member. Chomping at the throat as they thrashed with their teeth rapidly tearing away the flesh. Then when they smelled blood, the attack only intensified. She had lived through it firsthand.

Amari was the one attacked in the woods, yet somehow the entire town blamed her. Their eyes would watch her everywhere she went. Judging her for what they imagined she'd done. A snide comment from one person brought chuckles from another, which only encouraged someone else to say something. They would surround her—or so it felt—little by little they tore away at her spirit.

If she left now, Andrew would be their next victim. Everywhere he went their eyes would be watching him with silent verdicts. They would isolate him from everyone else. They would make it clear he no longer belonged. He would be alone. He would be the weakest member of the pack. Then, when the time was right, they would pounce, doing everything they could to destroy him.

She decided she would stay. At least for now. Amari turned left, heading straight for the Sheriff's Department.

# 26

Amari parked across the street from the Sheriff's Department. She examined the building for a moment as deputies came and went from the structure in a seamless flow. She wasn't sure how many deputies the department staffed. She thought for a town the size of New Hope— even including surrounding counties—it couldn't be more than a dozen. The department had not even been around when she was a kid. There had been a local police department, but her father stated the town could no longer fund it, so it closed. Surrounding counties were responsible for policing New Hope, which was not a beneficial trade for any party involved. Response times to New Hope were astronomical, while the number of calls coming from New Hope was disproportionately higher than some surrounding towns. Typically, non-violent crimes, her father had shared, still the resources spent on a town too broke for its department had not been a balanced trade.

He had not mentioned the state bringing in a Sheriff's Department, though. Then again, she recalled, she had made it clear each time he brought the town up she was not interested. Amari noticed the building was clearly the newest in town. The light brown brick still had all its vibrance. The green tin roof was untarnished by the sun but also unfazed by Mother Nature. It was unassuming for the most part. Had there not been a large white sign indicating the building housed the Sheriff and her deputies, it would look like any other business building.

Amari removed her Smith & Wesson from her holster then opened her glove box. Inside the glovebox, she had a six-inch by two-inch gun safe opened only by her thumbprint. She put the gun inside, latching it shut, then closed the door to the glove box and locked it as well.

Amari entered the Sheriff's Department, which aspired to be unflattering. She walked into an open area that would have become claustrophobic with fifteen people inside of it. Six hard plastic chairs had been placed along three walls. The fourth wall had large letters above a sliding window designed to alert incomers that it was the reception area. The walls were a bright white, with overhead lighting casting out an unnecessarily bright blue glow which did little to improve the grotesqueness of the area. On the same wall as the reception window was a wooden door where all employees could enter.

Amari was the only one in the waiting room, which relieved her. She wouldn't have to spend too much time— she hoped—waiting to get answers about Andrew. She approached the two-foot-by-two-foot window. Amari leaned against the wooden platform just beneath it to find the window unattended. After a minute, she knocked on the glass.

A woman in her late fifties came to the window with a snarl, condemning Amari for interrupting whatever she had been doing. The woman appeared to have given up on happiness long ago. Even though her work-issued shirt was black, stains could be spotted all over. The yellow embroidered Sheriff's Department badge had a blotch of some unidentifiable darkness. Her white hair curled in every direction other than where it should be. Her eyes seemed hollow. Amari could not help but wonder what kept the woman going as she leaned on the desk, with a grimace forever etched on her face.

"What can I do for you?" The shrill voice of the woman radiated insincerity in her question. She had no interest in doing anything for Amari.

"I am here to pick up Andrew Mathis. I don't know if..."

"Who?" The woman scuffed as she spoke the word. Amari had to admit the woman had made unpleasantries an art form.

"Andrew Mathis."

"Hold on a sec." The woman vanished behind the wall. She returned moments later looking more displeased than she had when Amari first saw her.

"They ain't done with him yet. You can call back in a couple of hours or wait. Just a warning, it'll probably be a while."

"I can wait here. Thank you,"

"Uh-huh," the woman huffed as she used all her strength to force her body up from its leaning position on the table. She grabbed a black plastic grip on the window, slamming it shut. The force of her aggrieved slam forced the window to bounce back so it remained open a few inches.

Amari didn't bother telling the woman about the window, for fear it may send the angry woman into a fit of rage thereby putting too much stress on her already overworked heart. Instead, she turned, walked to the hard yellow plastic chair across from her, and sat down.

Instantly the plastic bit at her, forcing her to shuffle her body to find a tolerable position. She could hear the penetrating voice of the woman through the crack of the window, speaking with someone. Both were hidden behind the wall, but her high-pitched voice carried.

"Do you know who that was?"

"Nuh-uh?" The second voice was deeper. Amari thought it was another woman. She could not be sure, though.

"It's that crazy broad who killed the young boy all them years ago. Mary, or whatever-the-hell."

"What did she want?"

"Her boyfriend is back there with the Sheriff. He killed the poor girl, Rosie, in the woods the other night."

"I guess the psychos always know how to find each other."

Amari felt her blood boiling. Every inch of her body felt hot as the arteries in her neck threatened to pulsate hard enough to rupture. She could've walked out of the building. She could've gone to wait in her car. Unfortunately, the thought had not crossed her mind. The fuming anger inside of her sent her sight red. Her ears began to ring as her temper grew.

"Excuse me, you miserable cow," Amari yelled as she stood from the chair, causing it to flip on its side.

The woman emerged from behind her hiding spot, sliding open the window another inch. "Excuse me?"

"Who do you think you are?" The other woman also emerged from the shadows to take her place behind the angry troll Amari had confronted. Either to get a better shot of the show or to make Amari feel outnumbered. Neither made Amari flinch.

"You better watch who you…"

"Shove it! I was the one who was attacked. I didn't kill anyone. Neither did Andrew. You are so miserable and pissed off about your shitty life you have to talk about other people you don't even know just to hope you get a taste of happiness. You're a spineless imp!"

Amari could see the shock in the woman's face, but it did nothing to dampen her rage. She was zeroed in on the woman, fully prepared to continue the barrage, hyper-focused to the point she had not noticed a deputy come out of the door beside her until he grabbed her arm. He pulled her toward the exit.

"Get your hands off me!" She demanded as she exited the building. She found herself standing inches from Deputy Williams.

"Hey, are you trying to get yourself arrested? You can't just start yelling at Sheriff staff members like that."

Amari bit her tongue before she spoke. "Her miserable excuse of an employee was highly unprofessional. Did you hear what she was saying?!"

"No, I didn't. I will speak with her about it, though. If you want to file a complaint, I will file one for you." Williams smiled trying to lighten the tension. "Macy is just a miserable old bat. You can't win with those kinds of people."

"I'm just sick and tired of everyone in this town thinking I'm to blame for what happened to me. Like I asked for it."

"I don't know anything about what happened to you. What I do know, it's never the victim's fault. Don't feed these people more ammunition to fire back at you. You're not on their level."

Amari felt her anger subsiding. A wave of calmness came over her, which sent a chill over her skin as her adrenaline receded. "Thank you. It does mean a lot to hear it from someone else."

"Look, why don't I take you to get some coffee? You can vent all you want to."

Amari smiled at the kindness. "I appreciate the invitation. I am starting to feel a lot better. Do you know when Andrew Mathis will be released?"

A look of displeasure crossed Deputy Williams' face. "They are still interrogating him. It could be a while. He might even get booked. Are you two close?"

Amari's senses lit. Suddenly, she felt the need to be on guard. She wanted to be careful of what else she said so she would not give Williams or the Sheriff anything more to pin on Andrew. "We're old friends. He is helping me get the cabin ready to sell."

"You know they are looking at him for some pretty serious charges."

"Like what?"

"Murder, kidnapping, and resisting arrest."

Amari felt the calmness fading again. "He did not resist! I was there when he was arrested."

"Either way, you should be careful around him. If he is the guy…"

"I guess you *are* on their level," Amari interjected.

"Excuse me?"

"You're doing the exact same thing she did in there. You are assuming he had something to do with her murder without knowing all the facts."

"I'm looking at the evidence. What do you really know about him?"

"I know he is a good guy. He was a great friend in high school. I know he has been one of the only people from this shit-ass town who hasn't looked at me like I have some kind of plague."

"Maybe you're stuck on the past," Williams pointed out.

"I have done quite well for myself, thank you. I am not stuck in the past."

"No? You are still letting what happened to you eat you from the inside out. You might not have the plague. I'm still willing to bet what you're holding onto is just as deadly. You are convinced Andrew is innocent because he was nice to you in high school. Your first night in the house, you believed someone was trying to break in. If that is not being stuck in the past, then what is it?"

"Where do you get off telling me what I am? You don't even know me, but here you are, being high and mighty like you have all the answers. You have no idea what I have been through."

Williams shook his head in agreement, acknowledging he knew she was right. He could never know what life was like for her. "You're right, I don't. You have to realize you're not seeing things for what they truly are. Andrew's knife was found at the murder scene. His prints are the only ones on them. You were alone in a house that represents the single worst moment of your life. You still see Andrew as the nice kid from school who stayed loyal. You still see the house as a representation of that dark moment."

Amari considered what he said. Part of her believed him. Had she imagined seeing the shadow run into the woods? Had she imagined being attacked? Those things felt far too real to be her mind playing tricks on her. However, seeing Samael in her car made her question even those all-to-real events. If she could hallucinate him so vividly in her backseat, maybe she could also imagine an attack. She reached for the back of her head.

There was a burning knot; she nearly winced at how tender the spot was. Did that mean it happened how she remembered? She tried to recollect if she bumped her head in the attic or running through the woods. She didn't think she had. As the possibilities floated through her mind, she realized she could not be entirely sure.

"You might be right," she finally responded. "Regardless, I want to be here when he is released. I owe him that. Unless you guys prove he did what you are accusing him of, I can't turn my back on him."

Williams pursed his lips, following it with a slight nod. "Your loyalty is respectable. Just be sure to stay vigilant."

"I always am."

Williams smiled and turned to go back inside. Amari stopped him without intending to. Her mouth opened without permission. She spoke without thought. "Williams, I think I will take you up on your offer. I could use some coffee after all."

His smile widened with pleasure. He descended the two steps he had climbed, walking down the sidewalk. Amari followed him to the diner.

# 27

Amari followed Williams into the diner. The establishment seemed trapped in some odd time warp, which left it helplessly frozen in the 1980s. The black and white checkerboard flooring had faded to a dismal creme and gray. Stools, the bar, and booths all had neon turquoise upholstery that appeared to have given up on its existence. She couldn't recall having ever visited the diner as a child, which made sense. The coffee wafting through the air smelled full-bodied, which promised a rich, invigorating experience, yet, she feared the consequences of drinking it.

As Amari followed Williams to an empty booth at the other end of the diner, she discreetly assessed each person she passed—fortunately, not many—to gauge their threat level. Some of them watched her, possibly doing the same thing, while others remained oblivious. Amari kept her eyes on the men a bit longer, wondering if any of them could have been the shadow she chased into the woods. Then she reminded herself that she may have imagined the whole thing.

Amari slid into the booth opposite Williams feeling uneasy having her back to the door. She preferred having a view of both incoming and outgoing traffic and liked knowing when someone was approaching. Amari decided she was not willing to share a booth with Williams as it may send the wrong message. Amari made a few awkward attempts to position herself sideways so she could talk with him while still keeping an eye on the door. It was uncomfortable and felt unnatural. Eventually, she resigned herself to sitting facing him, hoping for the best.

As soon as she settled into her final adjustment, a woman at the table. Amari nearly choked when she saw the owners of the diner were as reluctant to invest in new uniforms as they had been to remodel the interior. The woman's hair reminded Amari of a crystal blue waterfall as it cascaded over her shoulders, with streaks of white to accentuate the image. The waitress appeared to be in her upper forties based on the subtle wrinkles around her eyes and mouth. Yet, her eyes sparkled like a child who had not faced the cruelties of the world.

"I love your hair," Amari complimented.

The woman's face lit, revealing a set of slightly yellowed teeth. "Thank you, darling! My daughter wants to be a hairdresser. I am her practice head."

"Well, she did a wonderful job."

"I will have to let her know," the woman's voice was as bright as her eyes. "Do you two need a menu?"

"No, thank you, Doris," Williams answered. "Just two coffees. Mine black…" he looked to Amari to finish the order.

"Same," she agreed.

Doris nodded and gracefully twirled away from the table.

"Sorry," Williams uttered.

Amari looked at him with confusion. "What for?"

"For telling her we didn't need menus. I didn't even think about it. Are you hungry?"

Amari chuckled at the apology, finding it charming. Despite most of her trysts being short-lived over the years, she could not think of a time she had found one to consider her input in something even as small as ordering coffee.

"No, I'm fine. Thank you for bringing me here. Growing up, I never came in here. I don't think I even remember it ever being here."

"It isn't the greatest spot in town. But they do serve a great cup of coffee," Williams replied with an ever-widening smile. Amari could feel her tension melting away, which made her uneasy. Relaxing was not her usual state of being, but she decided it was time to ask the questions she needed answers to.

"Do you think Andrew is behind the murder?" Amari inquired.

Williams's smile faded, giving way to a seriousness that swiftly overtook his eyes. He leaned his head to the side, as if gauging how she might respond to his answer. "Honestly, I don't know. I haven't been working on the case on that level. I think there is a lot of circumstantial evidence that doesn't make it look good for him."

"Sounds like a diplomatic answer."

"It's an honest answer. A witness saw his truck driving into town ten minutes before the victim was probably picked up. His knife was found at the scene. The girl kind of…" he trailed off.

Doris returned with their steaming pot of coffee and two cups already filled before Amari could speak. "Just give me a holler if you need anything," then she vanished again.

Amari hardly noticed the woman or the steaming cup of coffee inches from her hand. "The girl kind of what?"

Williams took a deep breath and continued the thought after taking a sip of coffee, "The girl kind of resembled you. If you had blonde hair."

"What difference does that make? Andrew has been with me since I got into town. If he wanted to hurt me, he has had plenty of opportunities."

Williams tensed up with her words. "Maybe he doesn't want to hurt you," he argued. "But maybe he has a weird attachment to you or something. I'm just saying it's one more thing making it hard not to lean toward him being guilty."

"Tell me about the murder. About the scene," she requested, opting not to disclose she had already visited the scene. She wanted to gauge how honest he would be with her.

"We suspect Andrew…"

"The suspect," she corrected.

"Right," his tone lowered, and a hint of agitation sparkled just behind his eyes. "We suspect the murderer drove by her as she was locking up the boutique. Maybe followed her for a little or just grabbed her. Somehow, she ended up in the vehicle. She was then driven out to Skinner's Woods where the attack took place. Dogs tracked quite the trail, so either he let her out to run, or she somehow got free." He took a sip from his coffee prolonging the inevitable. Amari could tell he was dreading this part of the brief. She knew the images were raw in his mind. They would be vivid, at times exaggerated, making it even more difficult to discuss. After his second sip, he continued.

"She had tried to hide near a boulder within yards of where you had hidden. He attacked from behind, stabbing her repeatedly. He stole her phone, drove back to the shop, and called the police to make an anonymous tip about where to find the body."

Amari had more questions than answers as he spoke. "How do you know where I hid?"

"The Sheriff mentioned it on scene."

Amari rolled her eyes. The contempt was still fresh from the revival it had received earlier. "What was the rationale for him calling the police?"

"I can't think like a sociopath. So, I can't say why he did it."

"The feds thought it was the I-65 killer, right?"

Williams nodded.

"He's never reported his kills to the police. They have all either been found by hikers or in searches after they were reported missing. Why would he suddenly change his pattern? Why now? Why here?" Amari asked, knowing she might not receive answers. She continued without allowing Williams time to consider her concerns. "If it were Andrew, people around here know his truck, why risk returning to the spot he picked her up at to make the call? You don't think he would be concerned about someone seeing him?"

"Obviously, he didn't mind the risk of returning to the same spot where he picked her up to make the call. Otherwise, he wouldn't have used his own knife. And, let me remind you, nobody suspects Andrew in all those I-65 killings—only this one. Perhaps it was a crime of passion, a heat-of-the-moment thing. He felt guilty afterward, which is why he called it in," Williams explained.

"What the hell kind of logic is that? He would kill a teenager in a crime of passion? Now, that defies logic," Amari retorted.

Williams tilted his head mockingly. "If he has something for you, maybe he offered her a ride home because of the resemblance. Then, things took an unexpected turn. Maybe she rejected him or fought back, and he got upset. She jumped out of the truck, and he chased her down and killed her. He felt guilty because he didn't intend to hurt her, so he made the call to ensure she was found."

Amari took a deep breath, her frustration growing. "Those are an awful lot of maybes. What if there is another possibility you are neglecting altogether."

"What would that be?" Williams leaned on the table, clearly interested in hearing her perspective.

"Samael never died in the river."

Williams shook his head, regretting the decision to entertain a new possibility. "You consider it more probable than our theory?"

"You said yourself, she resembled me, and she was taken to the same spot he took me. She was killed just feet from where he almost ended my life. I find it far more believable that he got away and is wanting to get a second shot than Andrew coincidentally recreated that night when he was not there. A night he had nothing to do with," Amari argued intensely.

"I don't know why he took her there. We just know he did. Besides, I reviewed the report. There is zero evidence Samael could have survived in the river when it was as flooded as the reports say. Even if he had survived being washed down the river, he would have died of hypothermia."

Amari was about to counter by telling him about the cave and the sweatshirt she found, which she was certain belonged to Samael, but before she could, a man's voice interrupted her. She hadn't heard the door open. Worse, she had not heard anyone walking up to their table. She wished she had fought her way through the discomfort and sat in a way that prevented her from being so vulnerable.

"Amari, good to see ya again," the man said.

Amari's head spun quickly, her hand instinctively wrapping into a fist, but she relaxed when she saw John Meadowbrook standing at her seat with a brown paper bag in his hand, wearing a friendly smile.

"Oh, John, what are you doing here?" She stood and gave his hand a gentle squeeze with hers.

"Just came by to grab my lunch," he replied, turning to provide Williams a friendly greeting. "I heard about what happened in them woods the other night. I've been nearly sick ever since."

Amari felt the lump on her head throb. Then shook off the discomfort. "The young girl?"

"Yes. Of course. How are you holding up?"

"Surprisingly well," she lied. "I just hope they find the guy soon." She looked down at Williams with a condescending glare.

"Me too. It took me right back to there. Seein' you in the street. That poor girl." John's eyes began to moisten behind his trembling voice. He put a comforting hand on her shoulder. "You just be safe now, you hear?"

Amari agreed. "I will."

"Well, I better get goin'. It was nice seein' you both again."

John turned to leave. He walked to the door at a leisurely pace which made him seem even older. Amari watched as he exited the diner, then she forced herself to sit sideways in the booth

"Listen," Williams began, his voice suddenly seemed unsure, rattled even. "I enjoy talking to you, even though we don't see eye-to-eye on some things. I was wondering if I could maybe take you out sometime. Talk about things other than crime."

Amari's throat tightened. Her chest felt as though a large rock was sitting in the center of it as memories of her past relationships quickly cycled through her mind, eagerly reminding her how poorly they had turned out. She wondered if there was an ulterior motive behind his request. Was there a reason he would want to ask her out beyond spending time with her?

"I am flattered," she hesitated. "I will have to think about it."

Williams's expression showed disappointment rather than anger or hurt. "That is perfectly acceptable. At least it is not a 'no'," he pointed out.

"Thank you for the coffee, Williams. I think I better get back in case they've released Andrew."

"I will walk back with you," he insisted as he stood, dropping a five-dollar bill onto the table. "I need to get back on duty anyhow, or the Sheriff will have my ass."

"She certainly has a way about her, doesn't she?"

"She isn't all bad. If you don't piss her off," he bantered.

The walk back to the station was silent. During the brief journey, Amari replayed the last part of their conversation in her mind, concerned she had offended

Williams. Even if she ultimately had no romantic interest in him, he was the only person she felt she could call on in the department if needed. He would be one of the few deputies who would show up if she called in. She suspected Trishia had likely ordered the department to make her a low priority. If her suspicions were right and Samael had returned, she wanted to know she wouldn't be alone. Not again.

# 28

Amari found a bench outside of the station, nestled nicely under the shade of an Elm tree. She gave Williams a wave as he entered the building. She sat there for only a few minutes before the doors opened again. Glancing at her watch, she noted it had been nearly seven hours since Andrew had been dragged off to the station. Much of her doubted he would be leaving anytime soon, not if what Williams had told her were true. To her surprise, it *was* Andrew leaving the building.

He looked ragged, and she knew the last few hours of the questioning would have been the most intense. They would have been trying to trip him up, trying to get him to make a statement that could implicate him in the crime. Amari knew they would make him promises of freedom if he told them what they wanted to know—told them what they wanted to hear. Amari had used the tactics several times herself. For good reason. It almost always broke the suspect.

She was willing to bet Andrew had begun to question his sanity as much as she did her own. There was something about New Hope that seemed to drain the life force from all who entered. Of course, she reminded herself that not everyone believed that to be true. Her father certainly hadn't.

Amari ran across the street, surprising Andrew, whose mind took a few seconds to register who was in front of him.

"What are you doing here?" Amari felt a sting as the words floated in the air.

"To be here when they released you," she told him. "I wanted you to know, I believe you. I know you had nothing to do with what happened." She put her hand on his arm, looking up at him.

Andrew gave her a gentle smile, grateful to have a friend in a world where he found himself suddenly surrounded by enemies. He gestured with his thumb pointing back to the station, "Based on the way they grilled me in there, you're the only one."

"They must not have as much evidence as they said they did, or they would not have let you go so soon. Did you call a lawyer?"

Andrew shook his head. "I didn't know who to call. I have never needed one before."

Andrew sat on the curb, nearly pulling Amari down with him as her hands still gripped his forearms. She sat beside him, not knowing the words that could comfort him. She simply watched him, allowing him the space to speak when he was ready, which, fortunately, didn't take long.

"I just don't get why whoever did this would want to set me up."

"I don't think it's about you at all," she muttered.

Andrew shifted himself to face her. "What are you talking about?"

"I think whoever did it, did it to send a message to me. Why else pull you into it? Why else kill her where I was attacked?"

Andrew bit his lip, torn between dismissing the paranoid thought and struggling to find a more rational answer to the questions. The sweatshirt in the cave was easy to explain, but this was different. He knew this was more than a coincidence. Someone wanted to send a message.

"Samael is dead. Who else would possibly want to get to you badly enough to go through all of this?"

Amari knew people in town didn't like her. Some saw her as a coward, while others deemed her responsible for the darkness that had befallen their small town. Still, others saw her mother when they saw her. The woman who had crawled down the sidewalk slurring her words after she had smoked the last bit of smack she had. When they thought of Amari, they thought of her mother.

When Samael had been accused of attempted murder and, instead, had himself died in the woods, people turned against Amari. There was a unified belief she had to have done it intentionally, using Samael's attack on her as an alibi to cover up her murderous nature. Samael had been the boy next door, always eager to help a neighbor in need, the popular jock, as well as the kid who always aced his tests. In contrast, Amari was quiet, held a B average, and had little involvement with anything in the community.

"I think I have something at the cabin that might be able to narrow it down a little," Amari said.

Andrew's look was perplexed. "What could you possibly have that would help us?"

"My old stuff in the attic. Let's go. You'll see what I am talking about."

Andrew got up to follow Amari to her car. He hardly spoke the entire drive home. His eyes seemed transfixed on some distant point, perhaps wherever his mind had taken refuge. A place where things were right, where things made sense—certainly not where they were now. Even Amari's mind was not there in the moment as she drove. She caught herself stealing an occasional glance into the rearview mirror, checking to make sure he was not in the car again.

# 29

Amari reached into the glovebox to retrieve her gun when they parked, then slid it into her purse before storming into the house on a mission with a clear objective. She headed straight for the stairs, ascending them before Andrew could even ask what she was looking for or offer help. She stopped in the center of the hall outside of her room. She tugged at the attic access cord. The lid dropped, sending the ladder stubbornly downward. She climbed it without answering Andrew as he called up to her from the floor below.

Amari went to the stack of boxes which contained the belongings she had left when she went to college, which, she knew, was almost everything. She had planned on starting a new life, except nothing about New Hope would allow her to do that. She tore at the tape of a few boxes, relieved to find the fourth box held what she was searching for.

She squeezed her arms around the large box with a tortured groan as her body strained to lift it. The box had not been particularly heavy; it was the contents shifting that caused the weight to become unstable, making her muscles tense in ways they were not used to. She cautiously approached the opening of the attic, calling down to Andrew.

"I'm here," he told her. "What the hell is in there?"

"I think it might tell us what we want to know."

Amari slid the box down the ladder, careful not to tear away the decaying tape struggling to hold the flaps together. Andrew effortlessly took the box into his arms, holding it as though the unbalanced weight sat in perfect form.

"Where do you want me to take it?"

"Down to the kitchen," Amari told him. She went back to the stacks of boxes to be sure there was nothing else of use. Once she was satisfied she had found what she wanted, she descended the ladder, being sure to close the attic. Too often since returning did the need to double-check whether an entry point was securely latched play out horribly for her. It was no longer an eccentricity but a necessity. When she was sure the attic was closed, she headed to the kitchen to meet Andrew.

When she entered, Andrew was drinking a glass of water, his body leaning on the box, causing it to cave in at the top. He offered her a glass. Amari waived it away as if it would poison her train of thought. She pulled the box from under his arm, lifting the flaps, pulling out two scrapbooks that had been resting near the top and left side over the rest of the contents inside.

She dropped the two old binders onto the counter. The decorative leather around them began to fade from the deep brown it had once been to a lifeless tan with a stale look. When she opened the first one, Andrew knew right away what the scrapbook was. The first page was full of newspaper clippings from her attack.

"Why would you keep this?" His voice shook at the idea of anyone wanting to look back on such a horrible night.

"My dad thought it would be good for me to keep these as a reminder of how 'tough and unshakable' I am." Amari laughed at the thought. "If he could see me now. If he knew how broken I really am," she thought out loud.

"You're not broken," assured Andrew.

"He said if life ever got too hard, I could look back at this to remind myself I can make it through anything."

Andrew put a hand on her shoulder, but Amari could not look at him. She felt a ball rise in her throat, sparking her eyes to moisten. She did not want him to see her cry, not when she was supposed to be the tough one.

Amari cleared her throat and took a deep breath, forcing it past the lump. "Anyway, I highlighted the names of everyone who blamed me for what happened. At least to the papers. There are probably a lot more who never got interviewed."

Andrew ran his finger down each clipping as he flipped through the pages. Amari still could not bring herself to look at him. She kept her eyes low as she listened to him as he read the names. She could feel the anger in his breath.

Amari didn't need to look at the pages with him. She remembered all seven of their names just as clearly as their heartless comments.

*Judith Deerbourne*, the sanctimonious witch, had said, *I would not doubt it for a second if she took him up there under false pretenses. Tried to rob him or seduce him. She was the daughter of a druggie, after all.*

*Hank Miller* told reporters he thought Amari was high and had killed Mr. Skinner in a drug-induced psychosis. *Probably tossed the body in the river in a panic when she came to.*

*Margo Sandholler*, who was all too eager to say, *Amari was a rotten child from a rotten household. The whole family has stained a good wholesome community like a fungus.*

*Trishia Lexington* the one comment Amari never expected. *I always knew something was off about her. I can't believe I was ever her friend. She is a true manipulator. Sam probably tried to save her. Instead, he ended up dead while she is viewed as some kind of victim.*

*Meredith Skinner*, Samael's cousin and whom Amari had never met, *I hope she gets what she has coming to her. She killed Samael, who was the rock for our family. She deserves to rot in hell.*

*Cane Barrington. Something has always seemed off about the girl. You could just tell she wasn't right. Like her momma's druggin' rubbed off on her.*

And *Carl Goode*, Samael's best friend, *I wish it had been her instead of him. Everyone loved Samael. He was a nice dude. He loved everybody. She has never done anything for anybody except make their lives worse. Her own momma had to be stoned out of her mind to deal with her.*

Amari was broken free from the memories when she felt Andrew's elbow bump hers. As he looked down at her, he saw the tears welling in her eyes but the dam broke, allowing them to fall down her face. He brought his hands to her face. His thumbs wiped the tears from her eyes that she could no longer contain. For a moment, she tried to resist him but he kept her face in his hands, his eyes graciously looking down at her. She could see the fire in his eye. She knew the words brought him as much anger as they brought her.

"This whole fucking town deserves to burn for what they did to you. Every one of those people should be punished."

The harshness of his words had been undercut by the compassion in his voice. Amari had spent her entire adult life with those words playing in her mind like a mantra. The callousness of people she had considered neighbors, even friends, turning on her in that moment of her life had been too much for her to comprehend. She could not understand how they could be so quick to cast blame on her.

She had even wondered at times if her father blamed her. She wondered if her mother had used drugs as an escape. Not from the physical pain. Rather from the pain of having to deal with Amari. She had not anticipated the wounds seeing the article would reopen. How easily she could recall the coldness in the words written on their pages. The wounds had not simply been reopened; they had been torn fresh as if she had just read them for the first time.

Finally, she pulled from Andrew gripping his hands in hers. "Thank you," she whimpered.

# 30

Amari sat down at the table, jotting down the seven names from her memory onto an envelope she had found in a drawer. Andrew sat across from her, observing her feverish scribbling. She could sense his eyes on her.

"This is a list of the people who seemed to blame me the most," she turned the page so he could read the names. "Do you know if any of them are still in town?"

He read down the list of names. "Not off the top of my head. For most of these people, these interviews were probably the most they ever talked to anyone."

"If one of them knew I was coming back to town, they may go through all the work of trying to get me out of here."

Andrew gave a doubtful shake of the head. "Hating someone and wanting to chase them out of town is one thing. Murder is something completely different. As sick and demented as most of these people's comments were, I don't think any of them would be capable of murder."

Amari grabbed the sheet turning it back toward her. She scribbled off Trishia's name. "I think we can mark her off the list. She's a bitch, not a killer."

"Judith was old then. No way she would be able to navigate the woods well enough in the dark to do harm to anyone but herself."

Amari scribbled the name off. Then was interrupted by a wash of coldness. At first, she could not pinpoint the cause of her sudden unease. It came on quickly, without any warning, filling her from the core outward. Then from the peripheral of her vision, her mind comprehended what had sent her body into distress.

The motion-activated floodlights lit the exterior of the house.

"Looks like your coon friend is back," Andrew teased.

Amari stood slowly from her seat until she was just able to see over the window at the sink. The yard appeared empty. She remembered the raccoon. She knew the yard seeming empty meant very little. She thought she could hear the jingling of small bells, then she quickly forced the thought back. Amari no longer felt she could trust what her senses told her. If she had heard the bells, she would have heard them coming up from the trail. She would have heard them being removed. It was only her mind desperate to convince her the plan would be futile.

Amari looked down the hall at the purse near the door. She didn't want to waste time going for her gun. Whoever was out there would be gone before she made it out the door.

"What are you doing?" Andrew's voice sounded distant, muffled by the blood thumping in her ears as she reached for the handle, forcing open the door, then stepping out onto the patio with her hand tightly wrapped around the pen, ready to jab it.

She could feel Andrew behind her. "Someone was out here."

"It was just the raccoon." Despite how confident he tried to sound, Amari could hear the faltering in his voice. It was like a child trying to convince his parents of something when even he didn't believe the words.

Amari scanned the yard out to the tree line. She couldn't see anyone running through the yard. It didn't seem likely someone could get close enough to the house to trip the motion activation, let alone make it back to the woods, without being heard or seen. She had even adjusted the lights so movement would have to be within feet of the house to trip. Whoever tripped it had been close enough to touch the house.

Amari returned her attention to the lawn chairs stacked close to the house, near the trashcans. She felt a shiver with the tensing of her muscles when she saw the string of bells strung across the tops of the seats. She pointed to them, unable to articulate what she was seeing.

"What are these? Fishing bells?" Andrew walked up to the string of bells. He lifted them curiously. The minor movement was enough to cause a cacophony of metal ringing, which startled him enough to quickly drop the brass bells back to their resting place.

"That's fucking impossible," Amari growled.

"Fishing bells are impossible?"

"Being there is," Amari informed him.

"It's pretty smart," he mused, seemingly ignoring what she had just said.

"What?"

"Setting those there to scare the raccoons away. It's genius," his smile rapidly faded when he saw a blank stare.

"They weren't to scare the raccoon."

"Oh? Then what are they doing here?"

Amari finally brought her eyes to Andrew. She doubted he would understand her intent, but lying to him would be no good. He would see through it. He might even resent her for trying.

"I put them at the tree line because I saw someone run in there the other night. I hoped if they came back, they would trip the bells to alert me."

His eyes painted the confusion that had instantly occupied his mind as if Amari were speaking a new language. "I don't think I understand. Someone was in your woods? Why didn't you say anything?" He shook his head to make room for the rest of what she had told him. "So you set these there as an alarm? How could someone move all of these without making a sound? It's not possible."

Amari's eyes followed an invisible line from Andrew to the bells, and back again. "If they've spent the last twenty years being hidden it would be pretty easy."

Andrew's head fell in a slight tilt. For the first time, Amari wondered if he was seriously considering her theory. Amari could see in his eyes he was weighing, which was more plausible. Samael had somehow lived only to wait twenty years to torment Amari, or a real living breathing asshole had been playing a sick game.

Amari couldn't tell which he decided to believe. Either way, she felt comforted as he approached her. "Look, why don't I stay here tonight so you can at least get some sleep? I'll sit up all night to make sure no one comes around again." When he picked up on her hesitation he spoke again. "Or you can stay at my place. Whatever you want."

"You're too kind. I wish I had known how good you were back in high school. I might not be where I am now," Amari spoke with wistful desire. "I'll be fine, though. You shouldn't be inconvenienced because of me."

"It's no inconvenience," Andrew assured her.

"I'll be fine, I promise." Even as Amari spoke the words, she was unsure if she believed them.

"I can sit out in the driveway," Andrew offered.

She stood on the tips of her toes, gently placing a kiss on his cheek. "I need some sleep. Besides, I don't want to worry about you being alone outside. I will see you tomorrow."

Andrew waited by the front door until Amari was sure the latches to the doors and windows were secure. She pulled the blinds to limit visibility from the outside into the house. When she was sure the house was locked down, she gave Andrew a spare key so he could get into the house if he couldn't get ahold of her. Andrew went to his car with one final protest. Amari locked—then checked the lock twice more—before grabbing her purse so she could head upstairs for bed. She doubted sleep would come easy. She anticipated a brawl with the covers, followed by bargaining with her mind to allow her just a little rest. However, blissfully, her eyelids pulled with a contentious fight to be closed. Amari would lock her bedroom door, hopefully finding the escape of sleep.

# 31

Amari wasn't sure what time it was. She felt like she had not slept at all. There was a heaviness in her stomach she couldn't explain. It was as if she had awoken from another nightmare and was perhaps still in it somewhere. She didn't feel sick even though her nerves were firing sending flutters to her heart.

She could see a streak of light through her eyelids which only confused her more. She had left the hall light on. Amari was sure of it. Just as sure as she was she had closed and locked the bedroom door. The room had been dark when she went to bed. The windows were not on the eastern wall, so the sun should not have been rising into her face.

Amari listened for a moment unsure whether she should open her eyes or remain quiet. She had not fully assessed what was happening, though she knew she would never be able to with her eyes closed.

As soon as she decided to open her eyes to find where the light was coming from, she felt her bed lighten. It was as if something had been sitting on the edge of the bed near her feet and then suddenly stood. Her chest went cold as drums began echoing through her body up into her ears with piercing hums. She felt her chest beating with the force of a sledgehammer which exacerbated the flutters.

She opened her eyes enough to confirm her bedroom door had been opened. The light had been coming from the hall. Something else still felt off. She could only see part of the light bleeding in. She opened her eyes a little more before she realized the blockade in her doorway was a man in a black sweatshirt. The hood had been pulled over his head. His pants were also black. She couldn't get a good estimate of his height because he had already begun to descend the stairs.

Amari rolled over as quietly as she could to retrieve her Smith & Wesson from her purse.

"Hey! Stop, or I'll fucking drop you!" Amari threatened as she rose to her knees bringing the sights of her gun up high. Just as the front sight aligned with the back of his head, the figure vanished beneath the top step.

Amari leaped from the bed, dashing to the banister rail of the stairs. She leaned cautiously over the banister, making sure she didn't overexpose herself. She couldn't see the figure or anything suggesting someone was downstairs at all. Amari checked the bottom step. Once she felt confident no one was there waiting to pounce, she descended the steps and then stopped to scan the walkway toward the kitchen. The front door was still closed, which she suspected. She also had not heard the back door open or close. Though had he opened it when he came in, he could have left it open as he bolted out.

Amari was hoping for a fight as the feelings of violation pumped through her.

At the bottom of the steps, she turned toward the back of the house confirming, the backdoor was closed. This stopped her. He was still in the house.

The kitchen was darker than midnight. With the blinds drawn, not even the velvet hue of the moon glow was present to offer her assistance. She raised her gun again, ready to fire if she saw movement. She crept toward the kitchen, watching the darkness for the slightest sign of uninvited life. She stopped at the entry point, leaning her body in just enough to peer around either corner, feeling frustrated at the sight of nothing.

She crossed the threshold, where she was greeted with an animalistic growl. Her mind tried processing the sound but couldn't place it. She turned left, where the sound was coming from, spotting movement. She fired one shot before a thick, immovable force rammed into her chest. She felt her body become weightless as it seemed to float in the air. Then came the sudden crash into the tile floor as she slid into the wooden cabinets.

The air in her lungs exploded through her mouth. As hard as she tried, she could not breathe. Her head rang with a choir of bells as a sudden feeling of nausea twisted in her gut.

She heard heavy footsteps stomping down the hallway toward the front door. She heard the door open and then close after the force of slamming into the frame forced it back open. She didn't hear the latch, she noted. He must have picked them when he came in. She lay there for a moment hoping the stabbing pain through her torso would subside, and it did.

Amari rolled herself over to her hands and knees. Forcing herself up, she reached for the light switch by the oven. The more she stretched, the sharper the pain grew. Once the overhead light filled the area around her, she limped around the kitchen, turning on every switch she passed.

"Son of a bitch," she groaned to herself. The nausea still tugging at her stomach. A spiraling dizziness caused her to grab the counter's edge to keep from falling. Even then, Amari was not sure her balance would hold. She saw her gun on the tile but feared if she bent down to grab it, she would tumble over and not be able to get back up.

Amari looked to the living room. She saw the bullet hole in the wall, disappointed she did not also see a trail of blood. She had missed.

She felt something wet under her hand as she leaned on the counter. When she looked, she saw a dark red liquid sprawled across the countertop. Her heart stopped. It was a lot of blood. She checked her body until she was satisfied there was not any blood coming from an open wound. She looked down at the mess again, feeling her knees buckle as what she saw processed in her mind.

*Soon.* The *S* had been slightly smeared by her palm, yet legible enough.

It was written in some red liquid on the countertop. As she examined it more closely, she felt a slight ease in the fact it was not blood after all. Yet the comfort was short-lived because Amari had no idea *what* it was.

Amari spent the next half hour debating with herself whether she should call it in. She had reinforced the locked doors with some of the chairs from the kitchen. It did little to bolster her sense of security. Somehow, he had gotten in. Even with the doors locked. She had given Andrew a key. Each time the thought entered her mind she would fiercely wrestle it back. Only for the thought to return just as quickly.

At 5 a.m., Amari decided to call Laramy. She didn't trust the local Sheriff—or even the state police—to handle her call. The Sheriff's Department would blow her off. She was also certain Trishia had put a call into the state department warning them to not take her calls seriously.

Laramy was the only one she could trust.

He answered on the second ring, and before he could finish asking why in God's name she was calling so early, she purged everything that had happened the night before. She blurted out about the murder as well as finding the sweatshirt. By the end, she felt as though the two-ton boulder she had been carrying on her back had rolled free.

"Jesus Christ, Mari. Why the fuck did you wait so long to call me?"

Amari took a hard swallow, "I was afraid I would sound just as crazy to you as I do with everyone else."

"I know you too well. If you say this shit is happening, then I know it's happening," he reassured her. "I'm going to send Marcus down to keep watch on you. He'll stay discreet. You know the drill, keep his distance. I would also feel better knowing one of our guys got your back over that stick-in-her-ass Sheriff."

Amari felt guilty at the suggestion. Marcus was a twenty-nine-year-old Marine who had served two tours in Iraq. He would be security enough for her. He had also just gotten married two months before, not to mention they were expecting their first child. A daughter. Amari knew she could not ask him to leave his family for even a few days on her account.

"No, I don't want that. Although, there is something I want you to do," she pleaded.

"It is not up for discussion. I am not leaving you down there alone."

"I have some names I want you to run. I'll stay in a hotel. I don't want to burden any of the guys with my shit."

"Give me the fucking names. If you are refusing a protective detail, I want check-ins every four hours. You miss one, I mean *one*, I'm sending *everybody*."

Amari could only smile at his tenacity. "I can deal with that."

She read him off the names before she popped two Tylenol from the bottle on the counter.

# 32

As the sun began to rise over the trees to the east, Amari felt her guard begin to fall. She had spent nearly five hours huddled in the corner of the couch. She kept her back to the wall with her gun pointed toward the entry to the living area. If he returned, it would be the only way into the room. She would not be caught off guard again.

She had tried viciously to keep the nagging reminder that she had given Andrew a key just hours before the dark figure at her bed had attacked her. Amari's mind couldn't grasp the possibility he would break into her house to do her harm. If it had been Andrew, surely, he would have said something, but especially, he would not have attacked her. Her mind raced in aimless circles, always ending up in the same place.

She stood from the couch, trying to stretch the locked muscles in her back which spasmed in protest. Amari pulled her phone from its resting place on the coffee table by her leg, unplugging it as she did. She sent a quick text to Williams. *Can you do me a major favor? Bring me a copy of the police report from the night I was assaulted.*

Amari had barely put the phone back on the table when it beeped.

*Sure. What's going on?*

*Nothing. Just wanted to check something out.*

She waited a moment. When the phone did not ring again, she set it back on the table.

Amari wanted to keep her mind off the night before. The dark figure charging at her remained vivid in her mind. Every time she turned around, she saw him charging her. Except each time, the face, once hidden behind the cloak of darkness, became clearer. In the most recent occurrence, she saw Samael's face. It was older, dressed with a long scar running down the length of the left side. An injury sustained in the fight or the river, she reasoned. Her mind creating an image of what he should look like.

She decided to pack up the last of the linens so she could start going through the items in the garage to keep her mind occupied.

Amari had just finished taping the second box closed when a Sheriff Patrol Car pulled into her driveway. She guessed no more than thirty minutes had passed since she had sent the text to Williams. She half expected to see Trishia get out of the car ready for a fight, perhaps throw some accusations at Amari so they could haul her in for questioning as well. She also wondered if Laramy had contacted the department to let them know she had been paid a visit by an faceless assailant.

Laramy, she knew, would not be above going behind her back if it meant she would be safe. *Sometimes you are too stubborn for your own damn good. It will get you killed someday.* His voice was always calm when he pointed out the truths she tried to ignore. Always matter-of-fact. She knew he wasn't wrong, though. There had been times she felt the cold fingers of death just miss grabbing her.

Williams exited his patrol car, and relief began to flow through her veins, bringing with it a calming sensation. It was only a small comfort, though. She knew the conversation may not be a smooth one. As she prepared for the verbal tug-of-war, she found herself uncertain of how much more she could take. She didn't think she had another fight in her right then. She needed some time to regroup. She needed to get the image of the shadow charging her out of her mind.

Her back and head still throbbed if she moved too fast. She tried to choreograph her movements as he approached so she would not wince in pain, leading to his questioning.

"Moving right along, I see," he commented as he observed her organized piles in the garage. He raised a cream-colored folder he had tucked between his hand and thigh. There was hesitation as he handed it to her. "Here's the report. What is it you're really looking for?" He made no attempts to hide his doubtfulness in her reasoning, even before she spoke.

"I just want to see what the newspapers didn't report. I was so out of it when it happened, I don't remember everything about it." It was a lie she doubted he would question. His dark eyes, as deep and dark as a well, gave no sign of reservation.

"Isn't that a good thing? It's been long enough. Why not just let it lie?" He folded his arms across his chest. Amari wondered if it was out of habit or disappointment. Then she wondered if she had misread his eyes. She had a knack for telling what someone was thinking just from their eyes. She knew the eyes could tell a story as vivid as the most imaginative writer if someone were willing to look closely enough. With everything going on in her mind, she wondered if she had momentarily had a lapse in judgment.

"I thought I did. Then I came back."

"Well, I, for one, am glad you did," he flirted shamelessly.

Amari gave him a playful eye roll. "You like crazy chicks?"

"You're not crazy," his tone had turned serious.

"I must be to have come back here," she pointed out as she began flipping through the pages of the file. "Is this all of it?"

"Yeah, why?"

"It seems light. They must have interviewed dozens of people. Probably searched for him for weeks. This is only about five pages."

Williams leaned in to see the pages. "It was all that was in the computer. I guess it's possible not everything got transferred in. Or the previous department's record-keeping didn't give us everything."

"Yeah, sounds about right," she blew a sigh of frustration.

"So…" the words hesitated as they crossed the threshold of his lips. "I was wondering if you had time to think about my offer?"

"What offer?" Her attention was on the pages.

"To take you out."

This stole her focus. She looked up at Williams. "I still need time to think about it."

"No pressure," he promised. "I just want to take you out to a nice dinner before you head out of town. "I'm not expecting you to move in or anything," his playful smile made her nervous. If there were such a thing, she would have described it as a good nervousness. A kind of nervousness she had not felt in a long time. Where the fear was not driven by a fear of harm, instead, it was something else. Something less destructive.

"Okay, I will seriously consider it." She crossed her arms, leaning back, putting all her weight on her heels. "To be honest, I am seriously doubtful of a man who promises a *nice dinner* from this town."

He gave her a flirtatious wink as he turned back toward his car. "I never said it would be in New Hope. There are other towns in this world."

Amari watched as he got into his car. His eyes locked on her as he backed out slowly. She flicked the corner of the file with her thumb as the attempt to keep eye contact became too unnerving.

When Williams was out of sight, Amari turned back to the garage. She briefly considered finishing the packing she knew needed to be done. Instead, the folder in her hand continued to summon her. It called to her like a lost friend wanting to catch up on the old days. She decided the garage could wait.

Amari spent over an hour reviewing the five-page report. Most of it was information she had already memorized. The same information she saw in her dreams almost every night. At least recently. Her statement, her father's, John Meadowbrook's. The report of the scene and how there was no trace of Samael Skinner in the woods or the river. She could not help believing portions of the file had been removed. Either intentionally or by incompetence, neither of which made her feel better.

There was no indication they searched upstream. No interviews with his family. No information on whether they tracked his bank card or his parents' card. Amari felt hopeless as she scanned the pages. She had asked Williams for them with the impression it would give her some answers.

If Samael was dead—As everyone desperately tried to convince her—then someone else was trying to break her. Someone close to him was tormenting her night and day. That was the only possibility. Otherwise, she would have to admit she was going insane. Something in her mind had finally broken. She thought she was getting dangerously close to spiraling down a pit she would never be able to escape.

Whatever the answer was, she knew in the deepest part of her soul one singular truth. A truth so obvious to her she could taste it. She could feel its presence. A magnetic power over her grasping her, pulling her toward it. The truth was simple indeed.

She was going to die in New Hope.

She had come home to die.

# 33

Amari was pulled from her realization by the deafening ring of her phone. It startled her enough that the chair nearly tipped from her jolting body. She cursed herself as she grabbed the phone with a spiteful grip.

"Hello," she demanded without looking at the caller ID.

"Well, aren't you chipper?" Embarrassment washed over her at the sound of Laramy's voice. She needed sleep. She had once read a study which discovered lack of sleep could make someone fall into psychosis. If she had not reached that point already, not sleeping would push her the rest of the way.

"Sorry, I'm just a little jumpy."

"I don't blame you. I can still get someone out there. You can even pick the guy," the desperation in his voice thickened Amari's guilt.

"It's okay. I don't need anyone being put out on my behalf."

With a defeated sigh, Laramy offered her information. "I ran those names you gave me. Two are dead. One moved away years ago. Two are too damned old to be doing much of anything."

"That leaves two more," Amari pointed out.

"Yes, it does. One is the Sheriff out there…"

"Trishia. I know her. I ran into her the other day." She didn't feel the need to tell him much more. If Laramy knew she was spending time with a man suspected of committing a murder, one so like her attack, he would lose his shit.

"The other is Samael's cousin. Both still live in town. More importantly, both are young enough to be able to fuck with you."

"I don't think Trishia would be doing these things. Plus, whoever attacked me last night was much bigger. I would lean toward the cousin, maybe her boyfriend or something."

"Nothing came up on that end. I won't say it's impossible."

Amari bit her lip, swallowing hard, knowing the next few minutes of the conversation were going to cause her a headache. "I'll go talk with the cousin. I want to see if she still holds a grudge."

"Yeah, don't do that, kiddo."

"It's the only way I am going to know if I'm not going crazy."

"You know another good way?"

Amari rolled her eyes as if he would be able to see her condescension. "What would *that* be?"

The tone in his voice hinted to Amari he had picked up her disdain. "Leave town. Like yesterday. If you're not there, they can't fuck with you. If you're here, you have backup and they're on your turf."

"I spent the past twenty years running, Laramy. I can honestly say it didn't help one bit."

"Be that as it may, it's better than sticking around New Hope to get caught up on like you were last night." His voice pleaded to her. Even if she hadn't admitted it out loud, she had accepted her fate. Even if she were to die there—in the town that took so much from her, everything from her—she would not let it happen peacefully.

"If she's behind it, I don't think it'll be too hard to put an end to it," the confidence she projected to Laramy didn't mirror the apprehension she felt.

"What if it isn't her?"

"I'll cross that bridge when I get to it."

"Sounds like a good damn way to get yourself killed. I don't give a shit what you say; I am sending someone down there today."

Amari clenched her fist, slamming it on the counter. "If you do, Laramy, so help me, God. I will quit the business right here, right now."

Laramy was silent for a long time. For a moment, Amari thought he had hung up but when she looked at the screen, it informed her the call was still going. She was too ashamed to speak first. She had drawn a line. If she spoke, she would be backing down, and Laramy would recognize the faltering. The first one to speak always lost in the end.

"Fine. You hard-headed fool," he grunted before caving. "Okay, on one condition."

"I hate your conditions."

"You don't even know what they are yet," he rebutted.

"I always hate your conditions. They always mean more work for me."

"Well, in addition to the four-hour check-in, you need to turn the tracker on for your phone."

"GPS is hardly consistently reliable out here. Connection is even worse in most parts of town. What good is it going to do if it doesn't work?" Amari flipped through her apps to turn the locator on even as she spoke. Her resistance was an illusion to convince Laramy— maybe even herself—that she had some control over the situation. Or part of it.

"It will make me feel better. Okay, kiddo?"

Amari's voice softened. "Okay. I'll turn it on. Thanks, Laramy."

"Don't get yourself killed, or I'll be pissed off."

Amari laughed. It felt good. For a single second in time, she felt normal again. "I will do my best."

# 34

The house sat unassuming at the end of a long, crumbling driveway. It looked no different than most of the other houses in town. A single-family ranch home with stained paint surrounded by long-forgotten plants in the garden, begging to be remembered. The bones of the 1950s architecture had stood the test of time despite its need for minor touch-ups. Had Amari not known the year the house was built—because her dad had always commented on things like that—she would have never known its true age. The house had been maintained as most of the houses had been, with nothing extra having been put into it. She thought she had a faint memory of the house once being immaculate. Now, it just was.

Unlike the other houses in town, though, this house held tragedy. Amari was willing to bet no other houses in town had the family of a deranged attempted murderer inhabiting it. Amari had imagined the interaction with Samael's cousin the entire drive to the house. Talking with the woman she had never met, but who would certainly blame Amari for Samael's death. She imagined the faceless woman screaming, throwing threats, or simply rushing Amari to unload a physical attack. Each possible outcome can cut just as viciously as Samael's knife.

The words Meredith Skinner had spoken to the newspaper played like a scratched record in Amari's mind. *She killed the rock of our family. I hope she burns in hell.* Amari didn't know if the woman would still hold such a powerful stance twenty years later. She was not willing to doubt it. Amari would have to be vigilant. She was going to have to make sure she had a clean escape if she needed it. Amari took a deep breath as she got out of the car.

Amari could feel her breathing begin to strain, which ignited an uncomfortable pinching in her stomach. A cold sweat rose from the skin below her hairline despite the muggy temperatures, forcing her body to shiver as it struggled to figure out which temperature it needed to account for. She thought about getting back in the car. For the first time since becoming his partner, she began to seriously consider listening to Laramy. She wasn't sure how she was going to start the conversation, which made the squeezing in her chest double down. Amari grabbed her torso between her chest and upper abdomen as the anxiety sent waves of pain through her.

Maybe, she reasoned, Meredith would recognize her. The conversation would begin easily enough then. Though Amari was not sure if she preferred that more than Meredith not remembering her at all. Amari took one last hard breath before she went for the door, giving an invested knock before she had any more time to reconsider what she was doing.

A small dog began barking from the other side of the tarnished wood barrier. The dog's barks intensified as the seconds passed while the door stubbornly remained shut. The yip of the dog was piercing but not intimidating. She knocked again, further agitating the riled beast on the other side. After a few seconds, the dog yelped. Amari could hear its paws sliding across uncarpeted floors.

Two latches clicked in rapid succession before the door opened slowly, under stern protest. From the crack between the door and the frame, two brown eyes appeared. Both the eyes as well as the face around them were tired. They told a story of someone being beaten by life in many respects, though Amari didn't care to read their story much further. Random strands of honey-colored hair fell over the face without direction. It was an exclamation to the fatigue in the eyes.

Then the tired eyes seemed to come to life. Amari couldn't tell if it was because there was recognition or because the eyes had determined Amari was not a threat. At least, not yet.

"I'm not buying nothin'." Meredith's voice was as exhausted as the rest of her.

"I'm not here to sell you anything," Amari responded gently.

Meredith opened the door a little more, keeping herself inside. She wore dark blue scrubs, causing Amari to wonder if Meredith had just gotten off a shift. Her nervousness allowed guilt to fill in the rest of her emotional voids, draining her energy even quicker. "Then what do you want?"

"Meredith, I don't know if you remember me?" Amari stopped, letting Meredith examine her for a moment. Amari could only guess what sort of inventory the woman was taking, though Amari had taken one herself.

The tired eyes yearning for sleep narrowed after their second inspection. Meredith recognized her. Or, at least thought she did. It was clear enough to Amari as Meredith's face tightened. Then it relaxed. Meredith reached into the front pocket of her scrubs, retrieving a small bottle of vodka which she opened, then promptly finished off with one hardy swig. The tiredness in her face and eyes was from a hangover, Amari decided, not from work. Though, she knew plenty of cops where the two were synonymous. Perhaps medical workers were the same?

"I heard you were back in town."

"Yeah," Amari acknowledged. She didn't want to give Meredith the whole story about what brought her back. She guessed the woman already knew.

"Come in," Meredith grunted as she turned back into the house.

Amari hesitantly followed. She glanced around the entryway to make sure she was not being lured into an unescapable situation. The house was mostly well-kept, apart from a few stray garments calling the floor home. There had been a few dishes in the kitchen to the right of the entryway, but for the most part, Meredith's physical appearance didn't match the appearance of the home.

"Sit," Meredith groaned, pointing to a couch in the living room. The whole house was an open concept. From her position, Amari could see into the kitchen, one bathroom, and a hallway with two closed doors. She liked the layout because it allowed her a panoramic view of all entry points.

"Do you want a drink?" Meredith asked as she fumbled in a drawer for another bottle.

"I am fine. Thank you."

Meredith sat in the loveseat, which was angled horizontally on the left of the sofa Amari had chosen to sit in. Meredith cracked open another small bottle of vodka. It reminded Amari of the kind hotels stocked in the room fridge.

"Why did you come here?"

Amari wove her hands together as if washing away the tension pulsating through them. "I needed to talk to you. To be honest, I don't know how to even start without sounding crazy."

Meredith gave her a twisted smirk. "No worries there. I already know you're crazy."

Amari was surprised the comment did not bring offense. She understood Meredith's perspective. As wrong as the woman was, Samael was family. It made sense she saw the whole thing as Amari's fault. No one could ever admit their loved ones were at fault for anything horrific.

"Someone has been harassing me."

Meredith's right eyebrow rose suspiciously. "What does that have to do with me?" She tilted the remaining vodka into her mouth.

Amari wasn't sure where to start. She had imagined the conversation playing out her entire drive to the house, except in her imagination, Meredith had not been drunk. She had been angry and hostile. "I've been getting notes in my house. I was attacked in my house. They even took the bracelet my mother gave me."

"I still don't see what that has to do with me. If I'm not drunk, I'm at work. If I'm lucky, I'm both." Her words were beginning to slur. Amari wasn't sure how long she had before Meredith faded off into a stupor.

"When…" Amari wanted to be careful how she spoke. "When it happened, you told reporters you blamed me for what happened. You were pretty upset."

Meredith nodded in agreement. Her tired eyes struggled to track Amari's face. "I was. Honestly, it was such a long time ago. I worked through it."

"I don't want to upset you. It's not my intent. I just have to ask; did you ever hear from Samael after it happened?" Amari knew instantly she had found Meredith's line. She also knew she had crossed it.

"He died. You know that." Meredith's drunken face twisted into an exaggerated look of confusion.

Amari gave her drying lips a once-over with her tongue. "I found his sweatshirt in a cave across the river from where… it happened. I don't think he died. I think the cops just saw it as an easy way to close the whole thing."

Meredith's twisted smile returned. It seemed to be mocking Amari. "You don't know, do you?"

Amari didn't speak. She stared at Meredith, confused. Amari had talked with her share of drunk people in distress. Meredith seemed different. She seemed to know what she was saying, as if the alcohol had no impact on her cognition, only her physical state.

Meredith nearly jumped from her seat; Amari flinched back, feeling foolish when Meredith laughed at the reaction. Meredith stomped down the hall to one of the closed doors. Amari slid her hand up to the pistol on her hip. She suddenly regretted coming over. Nothing good would result from what was to come. Dozens of scenarios ran through Amari's racing mind. Was she getting a weapon? Was she going to attack her? Was she calling the sheriff? If Amari had to defend herself, how would she explain doing so in Meredith's home? Was someone else back there? Amari began to stand, hoping she could slip out before Meredith returned. To her disappointment, she couldn't.

Meredith returned from the room with a yellow-stained sheet of paper gripped in her right hand. Amari moved her hand back to her knee as she lowered herself back onto the couch. When she reached the couch, Meredith tossed the sheet of paper down onto Amari's lap.

"What's this?" Amari asked before opening it.

"I'm honestly surprised you don't know. I thought you and your daddy were thick as thieves?"

Amari opened the page. The words were smudged because the ink had begun to fade. Fortunately, she could still read them clearly enough. They didn't make sense to her.

She eyed the scratched writing, trying to understand. She couldn't identify the penmanship; it certainly wasn't her father's. Though, the way Meredith spoke, Amari felt the other woman did.

*Sam didn't die in no river. They killed him, sure enough, they did. Just not the way the police be saying.*

"What is this supposed to be?"

Meredith nodded down at the note. "Found the note on the porch two weeks after it all happened. Just sittin' there."

"Who killed Sam?"

Meredith shrugged with a grunt. "Hell if I know. Sam had already been dead for two weeks as far as I was concerned. This just proved to me you lied. I mean, I already knew. Just nice to have someone prove it to me."

Amari bit her lip, not wanting to sound too defensive. "I never lied about anything. I wasn't even the one who said he had died in the river. That was everyone else."

Meredith's eyebrows rose then they never dropped. "Doesn't really matter. Does it? I don't know who has been messing with you. I just know it wasn't me." Meredith leaned closer to Amari, the invasive scent of the vodka blowing toward her nostrils, leaving the air around her sour. "I also know it wasn't Sam, you lunatic."

# 35

Amari drove home on auto-pilot, navigating the roads through muscle memory rather than cognitive awareness. Despite the time since she had last been in New Hope, it was easy.

Her mind was too focused on the fading note, coupled with the distant memory tugging at the edge of her mind. She remembered a time shortly after the attack when her father had suddenly gone from on edge—sitting up with the shotgun, checking on her every hour—to being as calm as she had ever seen him, a glint in his eye she had not seen since before her mother's accident. Amari couldn't pinpoint the exact moment of the change, but it was as sudden as the world shifting from night to day when her eyes shut. She also remembered it partly because when he relaxed, so did she. She started sleeping through the night because the nightmares weren't haunting her every time she closed her eyes. She didn't know what brought the change, but now part of her was terrified to find out. Still, she was fully aware that unless she found the answer herself, the tugging in her mind would not relent.

Amari reached her house with her mind racing in hundreds of directions. She entered the house, locking the door behind her and double-checking it. Then, she headed up to the master bedroom. Her father's boxes were still stacked evenly in the corner, just as Andrew had left them. On the nightstand to the left of the bed was the safe she had brought down herself. When she had last felt it, she had felt something inside, though it felt light. The safe was open enough to allow whatever it was to rattle and shift inside.

Amari couldn't place the instinct as it screamed at her to open the safe. A conflicting instinct, buried deep within her, warned against it. Like two angels on either shoulder, one urging her toward darkness and the other to light. The images her mind conjured up of what she would find when she opened the safe brought tears to her eyes. Amari feared the memories of the kind, loving, peaceful man who would do anything for his family would soon be tarnished by a truth she was not prepared to face.

She steeled herself and made her way to the safe, placing it flat on the floor with the back against the carpet. The lock was a simple turn dial, rudimentary by today's security standards. The steel of the safe was thinner than even her bedside gun safe, and the bolts securing the door would likely shatter if dropped out of a window. The turn dial ran from *0* to *100*.

Amari tried her parent's anniversary. *12-22-82*.

Locked.

Then she tried her birthday. *03-20-89*.

Locked.

Amari then tried the date of her attack. Still, the bolts held steady. Then she tried the date when everything started to fall apart for the family. The day her mother had been struck by the car.

*06-25-02*.

There was a faint click from the dial. When she twisted the two-inch handle, the bolts retracted with a gentle clank. The hinges of the safe squealed at the inconvenience of being opened after spending so much time being dormant. Inside the safe was a single journal. It was a hardback journal the size of two card decks. It wasn't like his other journals. She couldn't recall having ever seen him write in it or any other that resembled it.

Amari opened the last page, then began to skim backward. There was only one entry at the beginning of the journal. Amari took a deep breath through her nose, not willing to allow herself to back out.

*It's funny what we do for our children. To protect them. To make sure they're safe. We are never truly aware of what we are capable of or how dark we can become when our children are at risk. I always knew I would protect Amari. I knew I would do anything to keep her from feeling the pain of this world. I never could have imagined what that'd entail.*

*Two nights after her attack, I grew weary of sitting in the hospital room. Hoses hooked to her while everyone is telling me, "I can't imagine what you must be going through." As if their words were supposed to be comforting. I would die a thousand deaths for them to never know how I felt sitting there. How my daughter felt. The helplessness. The hopelessness. The fear of the attack was only the beginning of the whole damn terrible hellscape to come.*

*She had been home a week when I went down to the diner for coffee. I couldn't have slept if I'd wanted to. Part of me felt guilty for leaving her in the house alone, but I needed the fresh air. If I am honest with myself, I hated closing my eyes. I would see her laying in the woods with the monster on top of her, his knife against her throat. I would scream for Amari as I tried running to her, but like a coward, I never moved.*

Amari tore her eyes away swiping at the tears with the back of her hand. Her heart began to ache for her father, even then. Once she was ready, she returned her attention to the journal entry.

*They approached me as I sat there alone. In case anyone ever finds this, I don't want to mention their name.*

*But I was—I am—indebted to them for all they did for Amari and me that night.*

*The diner was empty when I went in, yet I couldn't help feeling like the whole world was sitting on my shoulders. They checked in on me, and we talked about Amari and that sick bastard who tried to take her from me.*

*Then they told me the cops thought the boy died after falling into the river. They said search parties were all focused downstream, trying to find the body. Police weren't optimistic, thinking the swollen waters could have carried him clear down to the Wabash, and from there, only God knows where he could have ended up. This person didn't think it happened the way the police said. They told me they thought the monster had survived the river.*

*During the search that day, this person noticed a small row of boulders upstream. Even though the water had dropped quite a bit since the attack, they believed the boy could have used the boulders to cross the river. If he had, there was a cave no one had even considered searching. The way the person figured it, the boy crossed the river at the boulders before finding his way into a cave where he was hiding out until he could make a break for it.*

*I don't know how it happened exactly, and it probably doesn't matter. They convinced me to check it with them that night. If I'm being honest with myself, a part of me needed to know. I needed to see his face. I needed to ask him why he would do something so terrible to my Mari. Why he would try to take her from me? I wanted to make him suffer. A part of me wanted him to beg for his life, to feel, just for a moment, the fear that I know my little girl felt as he chased her through the woods.*

*We went out to the point and crossed the river. The water had dropped enough that it wasn't too difficult to navigate. The cave was nestled against a hill, easy to miss unless you were specifically looking for it. We turned on our flashlights and went in.*

*The Good Samaritan had been right. The sonofabitch was cowered in a corner. He looked like death had already come to claim him. He was fighting it off with all he had. The boy's lips were blue. He was shivering like a scared puppy, his eyes wide and skin I swear I could see through. He dripped sweat, shaking like the leaves in a fall wind. Likely an infection from the fight my girl had put up.*

Amari lifted her eyes again, fighting back the tears threatening to overwhelm her. She couldn't help but feel a pang of sympathy for her father even then. Nevertheless, she knew she needed to continue. She wasn't sure if she wanted to, but she knew she had to. If she stopped here, the Schrödinger's experiment would remain in effect, and she could hold onto the image of her father she had always cherished. If she continued, she wasn't certain if she could.

*If I stop here,* she thought, *nothing changes.*

The pages between her fingers called out to her, beckoning her back. She had to continue.

*It felt nice seeing him like that. Still, it was not enough. He was miserable, but was he suffering?*

*We approached the vile thing with vengeance in our hearts, or, at least in mine. The person with me put their boot to the boy's face. The boy crashed into the dirt though he didn't lose consciousness. It was momentarily gratifying to witness real pain on the boy's face, but it was short-lived. He smiled at us as he struggled to get to his feet.*

*That's when I realized how truly sick he was.*

*I asked him the questions I thought I needed answers to, questions I believed would help me sleep at night without the constant need to watch over Amari. Instead, he told me she would be easy. He was going to be remembered for the lives he'd take. He promised that, as long as Amari was breathing, he would come for her, find her no matter where she went, and kill her.*

*I'm not entirely sure what happened next. Something in me snapped, and I broke. I remember everything my eyes saw turned a deep, dark, vibrant red. Then, without warning, the world went black.*

*The next thing I know we are carrying his body through the woods. I had blood on my hands as if wearing gloves made of the stuff. The boy was nearly naked, wearing only shorts and socks. I struggled to hold his ankles due to the blood.*

*I asked what happened but the person only told me I had taken care of my business. I knew what they meant. Honestly, part of me couldn't believe him. I, a man who never got into a physical altercation my entire life, just killed a boy? It didn't seem real.*

*We took the body to a place where no one would look, where no one had any reason to be. We disposed of it in such a way that we were certain it would never be found, even if a wanderer stumbled upon the area. It was partly a selfish attempt to protect ourselves, but equally, it was a different kind of selfishness—to ensure that his family would never find peace, just as we would never find peace.*

The rest of the journal was empty. Amari stared out the window into the woods, struggling to process what she had just read.

# 36

Amari's heart began to feel as though it were on the verge of shattering. She hadn't felt as betrayed since her mother's death. Everything she thought she knew about her father had been a lie. He was not a loving and caring man; instead, he was a murderer. No better than Samael, hunting someone down in the woods before taking their life. Except her father had succeeded.

As Amari's mind desperately started spinning, looking for anything to make sense of what happened, she suddenly could remember the exact moment things changed.

*Amari had woken up alone. She felt a rush of terror as she scanned her room. Her father was nowhere in sight even though he promised he would not leave. He was not sitting in the old rocking chair he had built for her mother to nurse her in as a baby. The shotgun was nowhere in the room. Amari leaped from her bed, trying to call out to him, only to find her scream trapped somewhere deep in her throat.*

*Then she caught the scent of bacon wafting through the air. At last, she was able to call out to her dad. There was no response. The nervousness had dissipated, but it had not vanished. Amari grabbed a baseball bat her dad had given her when she was a kid. They played a lot when she was little, but she mostly played because he liked it. She never got past the boredom of standing in a field for hours on end with no one ever hitting a ball in her direction. She knew she would probably still have played had he not noticed she begrudgingly went to practices and games. Once the ninth-grade season was over, she never played again.*

*Amari descended the steps with sweat pooling between her palms and the neck of the bat. The scent of bacon grew undeniable as it blended with the scent of cheap coffee. The kind she thought tasted of burned water with added bitterness for taste. What caught her off guard, however, was the whistling. Amari could not remember the last time she heard him whistle.*

*When her mother was alive—before the drugs, before the accident—he would whistle* You Are My Sunshine *because he had sung it to Amari's mom every morning. Then, eventually, to Amari.*

*Amari went into the kitchen. Her dad was sitting in his normal chair at the end of the table which allowed him to look into the kitchen while also talking to anyone in the living room.*

*"Good morning, sweetie," he serenaded. As if he recognized how happy the words sounded, he tried again. Amari could never forget the smile that tried to reveal itself behind the words. "I thought you could use a good breakfast. I made your favorite: eggs, bacon, waffles, complete with freshly squeezed orange juice."*

*Amari could not figure out what had made him so happy. When she went to bed the night before, he was on edge. His eyes were riddled with fatigue. Though his eyes still looked tired, she could tell they had not been as dark, not as scared.*

*"You weren't there when I woke up. I was worried something..." Her voice became caught in her throat.*

*Her dad grabbed her hand and pulled her toward the seat beside him. "I'm sorry, Mar. I thought you could use some food. I didn't want to disturb you because you were finally sleeping."*

*Amari fought to understand his tone. What was there to be high-spirited about? Finally, she decided to ask. "Why are you so happy today? Did they find him?"*

*Her dad shrunk a little. He turned his head away as if ashamed, except she thought she saw a hint of pride radiating from him. "It's a nice day. I thought we could go to the park. Maybe take a hike. Or go for a ride?"*

*"Why would I want to go hike? I never want to go into the woods again."*

*"You don't need to be afraid anymore, darling. You're safe now."*

*Amari felt a tinge of betrayal swarm through her. It was not as ravaging as when her mom had relapsed— after several promises she would never hurt Amari again—but it had been close. She also noticed he had not answered her question about whether Samael had been captured.*

*"How can you even say something like that? They still haven't found him. He could still be out there."*

*She watched his eyes work. They seemed to be juggling a thought as if he knew something he could not tell her but wanted to because it would help her understand. He eventually decided on his answer. He grabbed her hand with a gentle squeeze. "I can't promise things will get better right away. I can only promise they will one day. You handled yourself. You don't need to be locked away anymore. Amari, your strength is undeniable. You can't let him keep this control over you, he's dead..." The declaration seemed so sure. So certain. "Live your life because you get to. Don't let him kill you now."*

*Amari nodded, understanding what he was telling her, though she wasn't sure how she could. "I will try, Dad."*

*He beamed. "So, what do you say we do something today?"*

*Amari nodded.*

*"Good!" He stood from the table with almost palpable excitement. "I will fix your plate. Then we can do anything you want. Anything at all!"*

*As he made his way to the stove he began whistling again. Amari could not figure out what brought the change. Admittedly, even she felt more at ease.*

Amari's entire body ached from crying. How could she have never, after all the years that passed, all her training, never put it together? His sudden change in mood, the sudden certainty Samael had been killed, yet she never questioned it. It was because he himself had seen to it.

Then a new realization pushed its way through. It was even more unsettling than realizing her father had killed a man. If Samael was dead—which she could no longer question—whom had she seen outside of her home? Whom had she seen in her car? Whom the hell attacked her? She had not imagined it! She had bruises; she felt the stiff weight of his body crashing into her. Amari still felt the hardness of the floor as she crashed into it. She still had the note he left!

She scrambled to her feet, wiping the tears from her face. She retrieved her purse hanging from the door hanger, then she scavenged through it. She had put the first note in her billfold just in case.

Repeatedly she searched, time after time unable to find the note which had so strategically been put on the table for her to find. The note was not there. The bruises and the bump were.

"Where is it?!" Amari screamed out. "I felt him. I could hear him fucking breathing!"

Amari collapsed to the floor.

*Have I lost my mind?* She questioned herself.

*It felt so real. It had to have been real.*

Amari looked back to the journal she had left on the bed. *Or, you've just gone insane.*

The note said, "I've been waiting." Samael was dead. She knew for sure now. Who else could have been waiting?

"No one," she whispered painfully. "You imagined the whole fucking thing."

# 37

Amari hadn't heard Andrew come in. She was intently focused on gathering her belongings from downstairs when he entered the room, but she wasn't startled by him. There was no reason to be startled any longer, though her anger had continued to seethe.

"What's going on?" He questioned as he watched her tossing clothes into her suitcases.

"I'm going home."

Andrew walked up beside her, watching as she continued to haphazardly tossed things into her duffle bag. "There is still a lot of work to do. Besides," he added, "you haven't even met with the real estate agent yet. That's in a few days, right?"

"I don't care anymore. I can't stay here," her voice was hollow.

Andrew grabbed her hand, physically asking her to slow down enough to talk to him. "Did something happen?"

Amari turned to face him. Andrew could see the fire in her eyes which Amari noticed made him uncomfortable. She pulled her hand from his, storming to the kitchen. Andrew followed her cautiously, then stopped on the opposite side of the island as her.

Amari pulled the journal from a bag she left, then handed it to Andrew before discarding the bag on the floor.

"What's this?" He inquired. His hands ran over the cover before opening it.

Amari did not respond. She let him read the words. To her amazement, though, he didn't read long before closing it and setting it down on the table. He let his elbows hold him up on the counter as he lowered his head.

"You don't seem surprised by what's in there," Amari's increasing anger transitioned from her father, whom she could not confront, to Andrew, who stood inches in front of her.

"He was supposed to burn this years ago."

Amari bit her lip hard enough she thought she may have drawn blood. "So, you knew? This whole time, you knew? That is why you were so sure Samael was dead."

Andrew nodded shamefully. His eyes were still unable to meet hers.

"Why the hell would you not just tell me?"

Finally, he found the courage to look at her. "It wasn't for me to tell you. He was supposed to have burned it. If he had just done that, it would have never mattered."

"Yeah, because as long as I'm in the dark, it doesn't matter. Right? I have been seeing things, Andrew! I fucking thought I saw him! You never even thought once, maybe you should tell me."

Andrew shook his head in regret. "He just wanted to protect you, Amari. It was all he ever wanted."

"He could have done that without taking someone's life. It makes him no better than Samael."

"He didn't know any other way. Besides, he had lost your mom not all that long before he nearly lost you. Then seeing you in the hospital, being so close to losing you, he went insane for a minute. It seemed like the only thing he could do to make sure you were safe."

Amari glared at him. "Was it you? Were you the one with him?"

Andrew jerked at the question. "Of course not. I was parked outside because your dad didn't want you to be alone. Trishia had her head so far up her ass, she refused to go." His face saddened, "They all did."

Amari knew what he meant. None of her friends visited her in the hospital. None of them called when she came home. When she returned to school for the last few months, they treated her as if she didn't exist.

"Then how did you know about it?"

"After your dad hired me to maintain the house, he came out to talk about some of the remodels he wanted. We got to drinking. I asked about you. After one too many, he told me about it. Said he needed to clear his heart before it was too late."

"Then you told him to burn it so no one would ever find out."

A dejected shake came from Andrew. "I told him to burn it so *you* would never find it. Because I didn't want you to think of him as anything less than you did before."

"That's such bullshit! You didn't want to be seen as an accessory after the fact. Who was it with him, then?"

"I don't know. He wouldn't tell me. Truthfully," he exhaled, "I wouldn't want to have known."

"I can't believe you've been here this whole time pretending to help me with the house and never once told me. Even after I told you what was happening to me."

"You didn't need more shit on your shoulders, Mar. Not then. Not now."

"Don't you dare call me that! My whole adult life has been a lie. You helped keep it that way." Amari felt the inferno within her reach the boiling point just before it gave. She grabbed the journal throwing it as hard as she could across the room. She jammed an accusatory finger into Andrew's face. "Get out! Get out, now!"

"Amari, please…"

She jumped in before he could say another word. "No, I am leaving. I don't want to ever see you, this house, or this town for the rest of my life. Nothing good can come from any of it."

Andrew swallowed hard, burying his rebuttal. Instead, he nodded, validating her request. He said nothing as he left.

# 38

Amari made the turn almost by accident. She had intended on leaving New Hope without stopping anywhere. When she ended up parked near her parent's grave, she was surprised, though not shocked. Part of her wanted to say goodbye one last time before she left for good. Part of her wanted to tell her dad what she had found. To yell at him for lying to her for all those years. He had promised there would never be secrets between them. *I respect you too much,* he had told her. *I hope you can trust me enough to be honest with me, too.* She had held up her end of the agreement. He had not. What was worse was what he had lied about.

Amari left the car running as she got out. She had no intention of staying long. The closer she got to the stone marking her parent's graves, the more nervous she became. Amari kneeled in front of the granite.

"I found your journal," she croaked. Amari cleared her throat before she began talking again. "I read it, too. I can't believe after everything I went through—after everything we went through—you would keep something like that from me."

Amari gripped the grass beneath her in her hands. She wanted to scream, even though she knew it would do little to help her. "All of these years, I was scared to come home because I was so sure he would be waiting for me. I was so sure if I came back, he would find me." Amari let out an irrational chuckle at the irony of her fears.

"When I finally did come back, I had worked myself up so much I nearly drove myself to the loony bin. Turns out he was dead. You never said a word. You watched me struggle, you let me stay away, and you sacrificed time we could have spent together to keep your secret. Why? What good did it do?"

Amari's head began to feel light. "I just wanted to tell you both bye because I will not be back again. Not for you, not for anything. I am going home to live my life the way I should have been living it all along. For the moment. Not trapped in this hellhole."

Amari put her hand to the stone so she could feel its coolness one last time. For a moment, she imagined her mom and dad taking each of her hands in theirs. It reminded her of when she was a child and they would each hold her hand as she walked between them.

"Bye," she choked as she stood from her place in front of their grave. When she turned, she noticed the cemetery was no longer empty. There was a white pickup truck backed close behind her car. She hadn't heard the truck arrive, nor had she heard anyone get out.

She looked around at the rows of tombstones in the area. Amari was frustrated when she saw no one. She suddenly became overwhelmed with the sensation of being watched. She could feel eyes surrounding her, anticipating her next step. Amari looked at the truck again.

"Andrew?" She asked with a tremble trailing her voice. "Are you here?"

She couldn't tell for sure. If she had been asked, she thought it looked just like Andrew's truck. Except his was loud from a rusting exhaust. Also, the door sometimes screamed when it opened. If it had been him, she was certain she would have heard it. Then again, she thought, could she be sure of anything?

Amari's heart began pounding behind her ribs so viciously she almost became sick. From her place in the cemetery, she looked out to her car. She had locked the doors—she thought. She couldn't see anyone inside, though she found no comfort in the fact. The engine was still running.

Amari took one more look around to make sure the cemetery was empty before she would take another step. A large maple tree blocked her from being able to make a straight run for the car. She decided to go wide of the tree so she could not be caught off guard as she walked past.

Then, hit with the reminder of her time there, she shook off the silly thought. The concern was unwarranted. A lot of people in and around New Hope had trucks. There were graves on the other side of the street. Samael was dead. She had nothing to worry about. She condemned herself for letting her mind continue returning to the idea.

Amari breathed a shaky sigh of mild comfort as she started walking toward her car. From behind her, a charred voice spoke.

"Time to play our game…"

Amari didn't have time to turn. She didn't have time to grab the gun at her hip or the flashlight in her pocket. A sudden sting in her neck caused her sight to almost turn instantly blurry. As her sight faded, she felt her knees quiver as her head danced without reason, causing her to feel as though she were floating.

Amari knew what was coming next. She also knew there was nothing she could do to stop it. When her vision vanished completely, she knew she was passing out.

# 39

Like a wave, Amari came back. She drew in a long breath deep into her lungs. Her body shot up from the earth beneath her. She felt the dirt entangled with old leaves fall free from her hair and shirt. Amari opened her eyes, rubbing them vigorously, only to find the world around her still blurred. The sun had set some time ago, she knew, because of how dark it was. She could also tell she was in the woods because the leaves overhead brushed against each other in the wind.

It was obvious to her that she had been stuck with a tranquilizer or sedative. She had seen cases where female victims had been given Fluothane, Neothyl, or Penthrane. Whatever incapacitating agent had been used, it hit fast and hard. It had also left a bitter metallic taste in her mouth as if she had been sucking on pennies. Her head throbbed as she became more conscious of her surroundings. At least what she could hear from them.

Amari could spot a shadowed figure several feet away from her. She couldn't make out his face or what he was wearing, just that he looked sizable. Slowly, her eyes began to focus. Soon she was able to tell the man was in black denim overalls. He had something shiny in his right hand which he twirled on the pointer finger of his left.

Seconds later, her eyes were able to fully focus. She recognized the man in overalls twirling a large hunting knife in his hand. John Meadowbrook approached her. She waited until he was within inches of her before she tried to attack. Amari, in her fog, had not noticed her waist chained to a tree just beside her. Though even had she not been chained to the tree, the sudden movement sent a crippling pain through her head causing her to dry heave.

"Now, now," he grumbled. "Don't go gettin' yourself all worked up before we even get started."

"What… What the fuck is going on?" Even as Amari was asking the question, she slid her hand over to her hip.

"You don't take me for some kinda fool, do ya? You think I would leave your gun right there for you to grab it? That wouldn't make the game very fair, now, would it?"

"What the hell's the matter with you?" The pain had begun to dissipate. With each second, Amari's sight became clearer. She could still feel her head spinning forcing her to close her eyes every few seconds to keep from getting sick.

"Well, that night I found you, Amari," he licked his lips as if savoring a decadent bite from a five-star meal. "I was born again." John plopped himself down into the dirt. He looked younger than he had when Amari last saw him. His face seemed smoother. His eyes were brighter.

"What the hell are you talking about?" She barked.

"Since I was a kid, I always had this desire to know what it was like to kill someone. To be able to hold their life in my hands, then watch as it slipped away when I wanted it to," his accent seemed to deepen as he fantasized about a memory. "When I found you on the road, it was like someone had told me, it was my time."

"For what?!"

"To bring my fantasies to life, of course. Then you went and said someone had attacked you. I could tell you were all used up. It wouldn't have been much fun to have my first time be someone else's scraps. Anyhow, I saw the boy crossin' the river when I went down there. Of course, the cops thought the boy got swept off somewhere."

John leaned in toward Amari She scooted back until the tree blocked her from moving.

"I was so jealous of him. He dared to do what I had only ever dreamed about. I finally got my second chance when your daddy was in the diner. I told him I knew where the boy was. Your daddy couldn't wait to go get 'im."

"It was you?" Amari saw a flash of her father standing in the cave with John Meadowbrook, ready to attack. She shivered at the thought. The people she thought she could trust the most always seemed to be the ones to cause the most damage.

"Course it was! Let me tell you, girl, watchin' your daddy take that boy's life lit a fire in my belly. Of course, I couldn't do it 'cause he was damn near dead like you was. Wouldn't have been any fun. It was so beautiful to see though."

"So, what, you've just been out hurting people ever since? What kind of sick fuck…"

John let out a grumbling laugh. "No! Seein' that fed my hunger for a long time. Wasn't till just a few years ago it came back. No matter how hard I tried, I just couldn't ignore it no more. I found me the perfect one for my first time. I could go months without doing it again. Then one day, I woke up and needed it. You understand me, girl? I needed it like I need to breathe. Like a man needs water. I *needed* to kill them. That's how I started the game. Eight have played. You know none have gotten away."

Realization hit Amari. She felt her entire body fill with disgust. "You're the one whose been killing those girls along the highway."

John nodded pridefully as he eyed the knife as if studying every bevel and curve. "Sure am. To be honest, even that gets boring. It's why I set your boy up, just for a little fun and all."

"So, why don't you just kill me? Are you telling me all this to just get your rocks off?"

"Oh, darlin', you're the grand finale. At least for now. See, once I heard your daddy died, I just knew you'd be running back home. I knew it would be the sweetest game yet. I've been waiting. I've been waiting a long time. Now, we get to play."

Amari's hand swept the earth behind her, searching for something, anything, she could use as a weapon. All she found were dead twigs and fallen leaves. "I'm not going to give you the fucking satisfaction."

John's eyes grew stern as his face twisted into a snarl. "Oh, yes, you will. Or I will kill that handsome little boyfriend of yours. That deputy, too. I will burn whatever is left of your life right to the ground. So, you gonna play, or you gonna watch a lot of people get hurt."

"Why wait all this time? You could have come for me whenever you wanted."

"Oh, your daddy was a stubborn fool, wouldn't tell nobody where you were. I tried lookin' a few times but the city is so darn big." He stuck his hand in his left pocket digging for something.

"Then why the games? Why fuck with me? You were in my house. You could have killed me then."

His lips curled again, the bloodlust in his eyes grew deeper. "You too smart to be this stupid. The more scared you was the more fun the game would be." He pulled his hand from his pocket. He had found what he was looking for; a key. He rose to his knees, leaning his body over to her.

"You ready to play now?"

# 40

"Now, I only got three rules. I can't change 'em 'cause I don't play favorites." John dropped his voice to a whisper. "Even though you are my favorite." He walked around the tree where he kneeled by the lock. He inserted the key but didn't turn it.

"Rule one, you get thirty seconds to run in any direction you wish. You can scream or shout if you want but ain't nobody gonna hear you, so you'll just be making it easier for me. Two, I'll give you two chances. After I find you the first time, you get another thirty seconds to run. Now," he flicked the key releasing the latch of the lock. John kept the lock closed to prevent Amari from getting free too soon. "Three is my favorite. The easier it is to find you, the more I'll make you suffer. You ready?"

Amari took a deep breath to prepare herself. *You're a fighter*, she heard her father's voice say. Amari nodded.

She heard the metal of the lock scrape against the metal of the chain, followed by the links crumbling to the ground. Amari didn't run; instead, she leaped at John crashing into his body with her shoulder. He let out a breathless grunt as they both smashed into the dirt.

Amari brought her hand up over her head and then down straight to his left eye. She frantically clawed for the chain. Her hand had snagged on something out of her sight. John wrapped his large hands around her neck. With too much ease, he flipped her off his body. He straddled her, putting his knife to the base of her chin.

"Now you only got fifteen seconds."

John stood from her and let her get to her feet. Amari was struck with another wave of wooziness, which caused her to nearly trip over her step. Then she felt John's foot interlock hers as she fell hard onto the ground.

"Ten seconds," he growled.

Amari forced herself to her feet and ran.

The woods were engulfed by darkness. She had assumed he brought her back to Skinner's woods, but she wasn't certain. Amari heard him scream out to her. He was coming.

# 41

Amari knew she hadn't gone far. She certainly hadn't gone far enough to confuse John. She didn't need to think back to her apprehension courses to know he would find her quickly. She could only hope he would give her a second chance, or she could try to fight him off. But she knew she wasn't quite ready, especially with how easily he had just tossed her around.

Amari rounded a large pine tree where she had been almost certain the roots were unearthed. She let out a breath of relief to find the roots were coming up slightly. She kicked the dirt and leaves around a bit to make it look as though she had climbed inside. Then she ran a few yards back. She slid between a thick patch of bushes. Almost instantly, she felt her skin itch.

Amari could hear him thundering through the woods. He was not as quiet now as he had been in the cemetery. As she listened intently for his crashing footfalls, she ran her hands over the dirt around her. After a few agonizing seconds, she found a rock. It was twice the size of her fist. There was even a point to one side. She gripped it tightly, knowing she would be using it very soon.

Amari saw the large shadow that was John stop at the uprooted pine. He looked down at the mess she had made, instantly turning his attention out into the woods.

"Guess you're smarter than I thought," Amari breathed.

John jumped down from the raised earth, where he disappeared to Amari's left. She took shallow breaths to avoid alerting him, though part of her wondered if he already knew. As soon as the thought passed through her mind, she felt his thick fingers wrap around her hair and pull.

Amari let out a deafening shriek as he lifted her through the bushes with ease. She could still feel the rock in her hands, though. She swung it as hard as she could. She couldn't reach around his shoulder as he fought her to the ground by the hair. She felt the rock hit something. John let out a bellowing yell and then for just a moment, he loosened his grip.

Amari was able to kick at his left knee, which brought him down to her level. The next swing of the rock crashed into his chest, however, his grip only tightened. He reached across his body with too much ease, ripping the rock from her hand. As if she were but an inconvenience to his goal.

"One more chance," he smirked.

Amari could feel her leg between his. With as much force as she could, she brought her knee up, connecting straight into his groin. John exhaled all the air his lungs had held with a slight shriek, like a dog that had just been hit by a stray ball. John rolled over into the dirt, allowing Amari to get free. She began sprinting in a new direction though she wasn't sure which way she was running. She thought it was from where she had been chained to the tree, which would hopefully lead her to a road.

"Last chance!" Amari heard his voice echo through the woods, already unsure which direction he was in.

She wanted to count how many steps she had taken. Unfortunately, the adrenaline pumped too quickly not allowing her mind to focus on the steps. She could, however, tell where the rocks and fallen logs lay in the path. She tried to stay on top of them as much as she could to not leave a trail for John to easily track.

As she rounded an unfamiliar tree, hands reached out for her from the darkness grabbing her. The hands twisted her, causing her to fall to the ground. She felt the hands wrap around her, lifting her. She began swinging at anything she thought felt human.

"Hey! It's me, it's me!"

The voice clicked in Amari's mind, forcing her swings to stop. She focused her eyes on the figure before her to find Andrew.

"What the hell happened to you? Are you okay?" Andrew asked as he searched her body frantically from top to bottom for signs of injury. Though she knew she had the signs, she doubted he would be able to see them in the darkness.

"Oh, thank God. How did you find me?"

"I went back to your house to apologize, then saw you were gone. So I went to the cemetery, figuring you'd want to say bye before you left. Your car was there but you weren't so I started driving. I saw the white truck at the pull-off then heard a scream."

Amari could see the fear in his eyes. She knew hers were at least as terrified as his. "We have to get out of here. Now! How far is your truck?"

"A hundred-fifty, two hundred yards. Your house is only about a quarter mile over in that direction," he pointed west. "What's happening?"

"I can't explain right now. We have to…"

Amari was cut off by a large blob wrapping itself around Andrew, tearing him away from her. She could see Andrew under John, the two men fighting over the knife John now held over Andrew's face.

Amari instantly looked to the ground for any weapon she could find. The first thing she spotted was a log slightly larger than a baseball bat. She raced to it, sliding across the dirt as she wrapped her left hand around the nearest portion. As she turned to help Andrew, she saw John push the knife into Andrew's side.

Amari screamed as crimson infiltrated her vision, just as her father had described about his night in the cave. Without regard, she ran to where the two men still wrestled as Amari's hands began swinging down on John as if she were chopping wood. She wasn't sure how many times she had swung before the log shattered. She knew it had been several swings before the wood exploded into splinters. Amari didn't wait for John to get up, she had done as she intended, she knew if he were alive, he would be coming after her now. If he was not, she would need to get Andrew help. Fast.

Either way, Amari knew her best chance of getting her and Andrew out alive, her best chance of ending the nightmare at last, was to get back to the cabin.

# 42

Amari could see the lights of the cabin less than twenty yards away. As she ran through the woods, dodging the maze of exposed roots and rocks, she checked her pockets quickly for her phone. He had taken that too.

Amari rounded the front of the cabin toward the garage. As soon as the door was within range, she brought her leg up, giving her enough momentum to drive her foot through the latch. The frame of the door exploded, sending fragments of wood in all directions. Her balance had returned to normal, as did the focus in her mind. She wasn't sure how close John was or how long after she had started sprinting through the woods it took for him to pursue her.

Amari dashed to the front left corner of the garage, where she pulled down a dusty tackle box. She let the box smash down onto the concrete floor, allowing the contents to spread around her. Almost instantly, she found what she was looking for. It was a rusted fishing knife her father had made from deer antler and an old saw blade. *Waste not, want not*, he had told her as she watched him sand the antler and then sharpen the blade, finishing the whole knife with two coats of wax.

The antler handle had a slight curve at the bottom which allowed it to wrap slightly around the thick part of her palm. If she needed to, she could hit him with that as well.

Amari went to the shattered doorframe, peering out cautiously to the woods. She listened to the night. Waiting. When she was satisfied he was not at the cabin yet, she crossed the short distance between the garage and the cabin. She frantically patted her pockets for her keys, again finding them bare.

She kicked the door just as she had with the garage—she wished she had the same momentum. The door frame bent slightly yet held strong. A second kick brought more bend but it held. The third kick let the latch loose, though the damage had been minimal.

Amari desperately made her way to the kitchen, where the entire room lay in shadows.

It was not long before she heard the heavy weight of John's feet thundering up the steps of the porch. She could hear him grunting. She thought she heard the dragging of an injured leg. She gripped the knife tightly in front of her, ready for the attack. Now, she was hunting.

"You want to play? Let's fucking play!" She knew he would struggle to decipher where she had yelled from. Her hiding place was shielded by a wall and a door. The hard floors would cause her voice to bounce from one surface to another. She heard him enter the house. He came down the hall and stopped at the kitchen. Then he took a few steps deeper into the kitchen, his breathing rabid and angry. When he stopped, she knew he was trying to pinpoint where the taunt had come from.

"I can smell you from here," he provoked as he added an exaggerated sniff.

Amari took a deep breath, which she held in the bottom of her lungs. She turned her ear slightly toward the door listening to each footfall as he made his way through the downstairs. Each one closer, much heavier than the one before.

Amari let out a slow, controlled exhale, then drew in another deep breath. As she did, she noticed his breathing was closer. She could feel his final step on the same floorboard she was standing on.

She gripped the knife tighter. Then she leaped forward. The pantry door burst open from the force revealing the large shadow only three feet from her hiding place. Amari stuck the knife straight out, knowing she would hit flesh.

John's roaring scream confirmed she had hit her mark. She continued the drive until his back was stopped by the island, sending him tumbling backward. Amari used the curve of the handle wrapped around her palm to help pull the blade from his shoulder. Inches from his face she could see his rage burning behind his iris.

Amari had just caught the glimpse of splotched silver aching toward her when she moved. She watched his knife pass her face and then dive into the wood floor. As he fought to free the tip of his knife, Amari ran again.

She made it only two steps before she felt the heaviness of his leg intertwine with hers, causing her to slam into the wall. Her face connected first, sending a radiating pain down her spine to her feet. She felt the cut open. Still, Amari stumbled up as she continued around the banister up the stairs when she heard the knife release from the floor with a deep plunk sound.

Amari slid between the crack of the door and the wall of the master bedroom. She simply turned so she could press herself to the wall. She hoped when the door opened, she would be hidden.

"You bitch!" His growl was deeper. "My rules now!"

Amari clenched her eyes for a moment. Her head was beginning to grow dizzy as the wound on her head throbbed harder.

Amari bit down on her lip to regain focus when she heard the stairs cry out under John's weight. The squeals seemed to be begging for him to move quicker; part of Amari suspected he could not. Before she could discern where he was on the steps the door burst open the rest of the way.

The handled end of the door smacked the wall she leaned against, forcing her to bite down harder on her lip to stay silent.

"Oh, you're going to be worth it all in the end."

The door had bounced slightly from the wall revealing John creeping toward her bed. His eyes seemed fixated on the piece of furniture as he twirled his knife in his right hand with hungry anticipation. John kneeled before the bed and then went to all-fours to lift the bottom of the sheet.

Amari attacked. She pushed the door away from her, throwing all her weight down on the knife, plunging it deep enough into his calf that she felt the blade slide from the bone. When he bellowed out a cry of pain, it was forced from her hand.

John rolled over, swinging his blade, opening a line of flesh on Amari's chest. She hurriedly rolled around to the foot of the bed to create distance. John forced himself up to one knee before his right leg gave way, sending him in an unbalanced hobble back into the hall. Amari saw him at the top of the stairs, peering down, his arms waiving desperately, trying to keep his balance.

She screamed as loud as she could, everything in her erupting at once. Amari reached the spot where the bedroom met the hall, and then she lowered her shoulders, throwing her body straight ahead. John's back buckled like a bridge under great strain.

John's size dropped Amari straight down from where she made contact. John twisted his body, reaching for the railing. He missed it by the tips of his fingers. Amari watched as he seemed to fall in slow-motion backward, the tips of his fingers slipping from the banister, John rotating himself until he was horizontal, then heard the rolling avalanche as he tumbled down.

Amari lay there for a moment, afraid if she stood, she would collapse. Her head felt too light and her body too heavy. She could feel the wounds on her head and chest pooling below her. She didn't want to look. Instead, she pulled herself to the edge of the steps where she could look down.

John Meadowbrook had landed with his back against the wall. He was sitting upright with the full length of the knife blade plunged into his chest.

# 43

Amari wasn't sure how much time had passed without him moving. She was certain John's knife had not punctured anything inside her chest wall, though. She used the banister of the stairs to pull herself up, the wound in her chest screaming at her as the head wound fought her resistance by taking away her balance.

She leaned her body against the railing of the stairs, slowly gliding herself down one step at a time. The knife, she confirmed, was fully inserted into his chest. It did not bring her comfort. She knew if the knife was inserted, the blade would slow the bleeding. She had seen several car crash victims survive hours with something impaling their hearts simply because the item limited blood loss.

When she reached the final step, she grabbed the railing to keep her balance. With as much energy as she could, she kicked his foot. Amari dropped to a knee, satisfied he was not conscious. She gripped the knife handle in John's chest then began applying backward pressure.

Before she could pull, she felt a sharp pain dive through her side. The burning pain swarmed her torso so intensely she had not noticed his dark eyes looking back at her. She felt his weight shift a split second before he crashed on top of her, trapping Amari between himself and the hard floor. Amari fought for a breath. Her lungs resisted every effort, seemingly growing tighter with each attempt.

John's large hands wrapped around the sides of her head. She tried to fight it but couldn't. He lifted her head several inches before slamming it back down again. Then again.

As he lifted her head for a third slam, she wrapped her right arm around his pulling him down and in toward her, forcing his body to move toward his right. Amari was able to readjust herself enough so when he rolled, his momentum pulled her on top of him. She pulled the knife from her side, against her better judgment, then jabbed it into his chest just below his clavicle. He rolled away from the attack forcing her second jab to enter his back.

John forced himself up from the ground with more strength than Amari could fathom. As she rolled across the floor, he brought his foot across her face. She knew he had not connected cleanly because she was still conscious. But the excruciating shot further opened the wound on her head.

Amari looked up to see John raising his foot to stomp down one final time. As the foot descended toward her, she slid her body, allowing his foot to crash down inches from her head. Amari grabbed his foot, hoping she would be able to impact his balance enough for him to fall where she would have the advantage.

Before she could, however, she saw John fall the other way toward the kitchen, as a black mass engulfed him. Amari could hear the scuffle. She could hear yelling. In her head, the words all seemed fuzzy.

Amari was able to roll over to her stomach and raise herself to her knees. She wrapped her arm around her stomach, using it to apply pressure on her stab wound. She used the wall to help pull herself up. She turned to see what was happening. Amari saw her father's knife on the floor between her and the two figures in the kitchen.

Amari grabbed the knife, then using the wall for balance, began to slide herself along to the kitchen. She saw Andrew wrestling with John. For a moment, she thought blood loss was causing a hallucination. Andrew threw a clean punch which connected with John's round chin. Amari could see the agony in John's face as the force of the hit traveled down his neck. He grabbed Andrew's shirt pulling the fabric violently, twisting his own body, then sending Andrew crashing hard into the wall.

Amari forced her elbows against the wall to propel her forward, then let her momentum carry her. As soon as she reached John, she raised the knife high above her head, then brought it down cleanly into his neck.

Amari collapsed to the floor only seconds after John. He was not moving; the knife in his chest had dislodged slightly. He was dead. She knew it was over.

She also noticed Andrew was not moving. What she noticed last was for some reason, she could no longer hold her body weight on her knees. Amari allowed herself to crumble. It felt easier. It felt comforting.

She noticed her body started to feel chilled, though not cold. Her vision blurred more than it had been. She wasn't worried or afraid. She felt relaxed.

*Welcome home.* She recognized the voice. It was her father.

"Dad?"

*I missed you.*

"I'm sorry. I'm not… as strong as… you always thought I was…" Amari felt the room closing in around her. The blackness seemed all-consuming as it swallowed up her peripheral.

*There's a lot of fight left in you, Mar.*

# 44

Amari crept from the darkness as the distant sounds of beeping tugged at her mind. Her eyes struggled to open. When they did, she found herself in a hospital room. Her shoulder felt as though it could not move. Her body ached all over as the rhythmic beeping summoned her attention. She glanced over at it to see her vitals along with some numbers representing something.

Her room was dim, which she didn't like. She wanted light; she needed light. Amari tried to call out to a nurse—to anyone—only to find her throat burned from a scratching dryness. The pain in her shoulder became worse.

Amari tried forcing herself up onto her elbows, but her body was too weak. It would not hold her weight as it quaked under the force before collapsing again.

"Don't move," a soft voice whispered. The voice was beside her. She recognized it.

"Dad?"

A gentle hand fell on her shoulder. "No, it's me."

Amari blinked rapidly to force them to see clearly. She turned toward the voice before searching to find the friendly hand with her. Andrew was in a wheelchair wearing a hospital gown. His left arm was wrapped in thick bandages.

"Are you… Are you okay?"

Andrew took his hand from her shoulder, grabbed a glass of water, then handed it to Amari. "Drink this," he suggested. "I'm fine. Had some stitches, docs said he didn't hit anything important when he stabbed me."

Andrew chuckled as he looked back toward the door. "I bet the nurse won't be too happy if she finds me in here, though."

"You saved me," Amari responded lethargically as Andrew took her now empty glass. He filled it again, tilting the cup to help her drink without spilling it on herself.

"You saved yourself. I was just there for the end of it."

"How did we get here?"

"When I came to in the woods, I went back to my truck to go to your cabin. I called the police on the way. Not sure when they got there. I just remember being rolled out in front of you before they shoved me into an ambulance."

Amari felt a sudden rush of panic. "Is he…"

Andrew pulled the glass from her to keep it from spilling and put his bandaged arm reassuringly on her shoulder. "Yes, I already asked. You got him." Andrew returned the glass to its tray then looked to Amari. "Did he say why he did it?"

Amari nodded through the pain. "He was always a sick bastard. This was all a game to him."

"I'm glad you're okay," Andrew grinned.

"Right back at'cha." She felt her eyes want to retreat from his. "Sorry for my outburst. I was wrong."

"No, I get it. You were pissed. I would have been too." Andrew sat quietly for a moment before he finally asked, "What are your plans now?"

Amari shrugged. For the first time in her adult life, she was not afraid. She felt content—though uncomfortable— with where she was. "Maybe I'll wait to sell the house. Might even stick around for a while. I know Laramy won't let me work looking like this."

"Who is Laramy?" Andrew asked with concern hanging on the edge of his voice.

"My business partner. We run the agency together."

"Oh," Andrew said pleased. "Well, in that case, maybe when you are feeling better, I can take you out to dinner?"

"Like a date?"

"Yes. Like a proper date."

Amari wasn't sure if it was the drugs she had probably been pumped with or if she was finally ready. She didn't question it, though. "Absolutely."

Andrew beamed as he put his hand on her shoulder one last time. "I better let you rest. I'll come to see you in a few hours."

Amari reached for his hand but the strength was not there. "Andrew," she called as he spun his wheelchair.

"Yeah?" He stopped to look at her.

"Thank you."

Andrew smiled, rolling himself out into the hall.

Instantly replacing Andrew was a nurse entering the room. Amari thought the woman looked like a piece of yarn in her white scrubs, barely small enough for her gangly body to hold. She went with purpose to Amari's IV where she inserted a syringe, driving a clear fluid into the line.

"What is that?" Amari asked.

"Morphine," the nurse responded with a wide smile. "I just wanted to let you know you're a real hero."

"What are you talking about?"

"Everyone is talking about it. It's all over the news. CNN, Fox, and all the local stuff, too. You stopped the I-65 killer."

*Great*, Amari thought. She didn't know where her phone was. She was certain Laramy would be calling and texting incessantly until she found it. If she ever did.

Since Amari had woken up, everything about the hospital room felt like déjà vu. Except this time, people were proud of her. They were honoring her. She was not the one the town blamed.

"Would you like me to turn it on for you?" The nurse asked quizzically. A little too excited, too, Amari thought.

"No, that's okay. I think I'm going to get some more sleep."

The nurse pouted. "You've been asleep almost twenty-four hours. I know the doctors want to talk with you before too long."

Amari nodded. "I'll talk with them. I'd rather just enjoy the quiet over the news."

The nurse nodded as if she understood, though Amari knew she didn't. She never could.

As the nurse left, Amari felt her eyes tug for sleep. Moments later—or at least what felt like moments—she heard a new voice.

"Amari?"

Amari opened her eyes to see Trishia Lexington standing in her doorway. Amari knew she had slept because the sun had started to rise.

Amari scoffed, the pain only muffled as the shot of morphine she received sometime between falling asleep and then wore off. "I swear to God, I was the victim this time, *too*."

Trishia gave a guilty grin. "I know. I'm not here to be a bitch. Just to get your statement."

"Can we do it later? I'm tired," Amari quipped.

"You know as well as I do; the sooner we get it, the more accurate it will be."

Amari said nothing. She just gazed at Trishia. Amari noticed the look on her old friend's face. A look of regret. Amari knew the look well because of how many times she had seen it in her mirror.

"I'm so sorry, Mar. I was a bitch back then; I know I was. I should've been there beside you. You needed it more then, than ever before."

"Then why weren't you?"

Trishia shook her head shamefully. "Couldn't tell you. I guess I was hurt because you knew I liked him. I was afraid because it could've been me, except, I wouldn't have had the same courage as you to fight back. I was too much of a chicken to stand up for you when everyone else turned their backs. I was stupid. Plain and simple."

Amari noticed a tear in Trishia's eyes. Amari nodded, wishing she could reach out and grab her old friend's hand. "Thank you, Trish. It means a lot hearing that from you."

Trishia nodded shamefully as she wiped the tears from her eyes. She cleared her throat. "I'll let you get some rest, then. I'll come back in a few hours after you've got some more sleep. You can give me your statement then."

Amari gave a thankful nod as Trishia left. Amari laid back in her bed alone, listening to the symphony of machines, disappointed she had found herself there twice. This time, though, she was not being persecuted. This time she felt at peace.

This time she felt safe.

# About the author

Jack Lawrence was a therapist in Indiana before becoming an author. He specialized in families and couples and did a lot of work with clients suffering from addiction. He currently lives in Indiana with his family and their dog. His debut novel, *Blood Thorn* was a first-place 2023 BookFest Award Winner. Both books in the David Thorne series have been Ingram Bestsellers.

# Follow Jack on Social Media:

## Facebook

## Instagram

Jacklawrencewriting.com